NOTCHES

ALSO BY PETER BOWEN

Wolf, No Wolf
Specimen Song
Coyote Wind

Imperial Kelly
Kelly Blue
Yellowstone Kelly

NOTCHES

A GABRIEL DU PRÉ MYSTERY

Peter Bowen

St. Martin's Press
New York

Library of Congress Cataloging-in-Publication Data

Bowen, Peter.
    Notches : a Gabriel Du Pré mystery / by Peter Bowen.—1st. ed.
       p.   cm.
    ISBN 0-312-15181-0
    I. Title.
    PS3552.O866N68   1997
    813'.54—dc20   96-30647
                                                    CIP

First Edition: February 1997

10 9 8 7 6 5 4 3 2 1

For the women who are lost in the desert

NOTCHES

❧ CHAPTER 1 ❧

This terrible, Du Pré," said Madelaine. She was looking at the newspaper. "Person, do this, pretty far from God, yes?"

Du Pré nodded. He sipped his coffee. They were sitting in Madelaine's kitchen. The breakfast dishes were piled on the sideboard next to the sink.

Du Pré watched the cluster flies fumble clumsily against the window glass. It was spring and the fat-bodied black insects were crawling out toward the warmth. They wintered in the walls of the house.

Madelaine handed the front section of the paper to Du Pré. He looked at the headline.

FIFTH VICTIM FOUND

Du Pré sighed.

"It is a long way from here," he said. "Pretty ugly, this."

"Not so far," said Madelaine. "It is what, a hundred miles, maybe. Just up above the Wolf Mountains, here, on that Hi-Line." Highway 2, which runs fifty miles south of Canada all across Montana. North Dakota. Ends at Sault-Ste.-Marie in Michigan.

"The parents, these girls," said Madelaine. "Oh, they must weep."

Oh, yes, Du Pré thought, your little girl she quarrel with you and she run away. Someone take her and rape her and torture her and kill her and dump her body out in the sagebrush, let the coyotes and ravens eat what is left, well . . . he thought of his two daughters. His grandchildren. Anybody's children.

"People kill people, here," said Madelaine. "They got a reason. Not a good reason, there is never no good reason, kill someone."

Yes there is, Du Pré thought, but me, I will not argue this time.

"That Lucky," said Madelaine. "He kill all those Indian women,

1

Canada, that Washington, D.C. What was he like, there?"

Before I kill him? thought Du Pré. Damn, him I almost forgot. No, I did not. Hit him with a stone from a slingshot, he fall and break his fucking neck so I don't got to cut his throat. Only good thing he did, me.

Du Pré sipped his coffee.

"Hey, Du Pré," said Madelaine. "I lose my voice? You gone deaf? I ask you this question, you hear me? What this Lucky was like?"

"Him, he was a bastard," said Du Pré. "He don't look crazy, though. Good thing he break his neck, he go to trial, they say him crazy, he be out by now. Give him Social Security or something."

My Madelaine, she does not think there are bad people in this world. Just people who are far from God. I wish she was right.

Madelaine was fiddling with the thick braid of black hair she wore, shot with silver now. Her face was smooth and unlined. She was still a little asleep. Du Pré lifted his coffee, and he smelled her on his hand. He remembered her in the night.

Du Pré looked at her, smiling a little.

"Eh, Du Pré," said Madelaine. "You want to go back to bed, now, you look at me like that. It is on your forehead. No. I got to go to the church. See Father Van Den Heuvel. No, Du Pré, you are a big boy, you wait till tonight."

Du Pré grinned.

"OK," said Madelaine. "This afternoon maybe, but not now, no."

Du Pré stood up and he went around the table.

"I bite you," said Madelaine. "I am not fooling you. Men. You are supposed, not want that so much, you get to be a grandfather."

Du Pré rubbed her shoulders through the thick silk bathrobe she wore.

"I am not explaining, Father Van Den Heuvel, I am late, our meeting, I am fucking that Du Pré. We are not even married."

We would be, Du Pré thought, you were not waiting on that fool Church say, OK, your husband, he is dead, you can marry Du Pré now. Eight years I wait for her to get word from those priests, something is stuck in the works.

Du Pré looked out the kitchen window toward the fields that lay right at the edge of the little town. Stout rows of winter wheat rose green above the brown earth. Tough plants, that winter wheat, stayed green right under the snow. Got a jump on growing in the spring.

Du Pré made a grab for Madelaine's ass when she got up. She slapped his hand and smiled at him, wagged her finger.

"I take care of you, later," said Madelaine, heading off to the bath.

Du Pré heard the water start. He got another cup of coffee and he brought it back to the table.

The newspaper. He hadn't read the article.

He didn't want to read the article.

Something itched in the back of his mind.

Me, I am going to get tangled up in this, he thought.

A warm wet scent of flowers and herbs bloomed in the kitchen. The potpourri that Madelaine made and put into the soap that she made from fat and ashes and berries. Métis' soap. Kind of soap Madelaine's old aunties, grandmothers made.

She always smelled wonderful.

Du Pré lifted his coffee cup again and sniffed his hand, smelled his woman.

This afternoon, he thought, it is a long time till this afternoon.

Du Pré looked at the photograph. Some people carrying a black body bag out of the sagebrush.

The body had been found by a rancher. The man had been driving along and a hubcap had fallen off and sailed out into the sagebrush. On the open range. The rancher backed the car up and he walked out into the sagebrush and he found the body. It was badly decomposed, the paper said. Evidence indicated that the murderer was the same person who had killed four other young women and left their bodies in places where they might lie for a long time, or forever.

Damn, thought Du Pré, there maybe are a lot more dead girls out there. Maybe, hah. There are plenty dead girls out there. This guy, he has been doing this for a long time. Like that guy Bundy, he killed . . . sixty women? Maybe more.

Serial killers, always men.

Hunters. But they don't eat what they kill.

Damn, this guy, he is driving in places which don't got so much traffic and someone has seen this guy, seen what he drives.

They see this guy, what he drives, don't think nothing of it.

Cut it out, Du Pré thought, you are not a part of this. No part. Ah, shit, I better go and see Benetsee. See what he dreams.

The shower stopped. Du Pré went to the hallway and he stood there. Madelaine came out, naked, wringing the water out of her hair with a heavy towel. Du Pré looked at her.

This afternoon.

I cancel, all them appointments.

The telephone rang. Madelaine picked it up in the bedroom.

"Hey, Du Pré," she called. "It is that Benny Klein."

Benny Klein, the Sheriff. One of Du Pré's friends. His wife owned the bar in Toussaint.

Du Pré didn't want to pick up the telephone.

He went to the living room.

"Yah," said Du Pré.

"Du Pré?" said Benny. His voice was distorted. So he was calling the dispatch office and they patched him onto the telephone line.

"Yah, it is me," said Du Pré.

"You see this morning's paper?" he said.

"Yah," said Du Pré. I don't want this, I want to fuck my Madelaine this afternoon, maybe take her to the bar, buy her a pink wine, a cheeseburger. Maybe we dance.

"Well," said Benny, "I got another one and this one is ours."

How do I know this? Du Pré thought.

"Shit," said Du Pré.

"If I sound funny," said Benny Klein, "it's because I just threw up."

"Where are you?" said Du Pré.

"The old highway," said Benny, "about a mile past the Grange Hall on Palmer Creek. You know the one?"

"Yah," said Du Pré.

"This is bad," said Benny.

"Look," said Du Pré. "You stay there and I will come. You call anyone else?"

"Not yet," said Benny. "Who would I call?"

"The coroner."

"He quit," said Benny. "So I'm the coroner."

Benny is a brave man who does not like dead bodies or bad people at all and he is afraid of much but he still does what he said he would do. Be a sheriff. He is a brave man. He hates it. He still does it.

"Ah," said Du Pré. "You call your dispatcher, have her call the State."

"I shoulda done that already," said Benny, "I'm just upset."

"I be there, right away," said Du Pré.

Benny rang off.

Du Pré walked back down the hallway. Madelaine was sitting at her little vanity, putting lipstick on. She was still naked.

"Hey," said Du Pré from the doorway. "I got to go. Benny wants me."

"He find a girl's body," said Madelaine. "I knew he would. Poor girl."

"I am sorry," said Du Pré.

"No," said Madelaine, "You are not sorry, Du Pré, you are my good Métis man. I know you."

Du Pré shrugged.

"You make my babies safe," said Madelaine. "You make everybody's safe again, Du Pré."

"I don't know," said Du Pré.

"I do," said Madelaine.

❧ CHAPTER 2 ❧

Du Pré shot down the old highway, driving ninety. His old police cruiser was still plenty fast, and he had very good tires on it. The lights and siren were gone. He tried to remember if this was the fourth or the third one that he had owned.

That Bart, Du Pré thought, my rich friend, he try to give me a Land Rover. I find out they are sixty thousand dollars, I tell him no good Métis drive a car cost more than three houses cost here. So he find me this. It is faster than all the others.

Du Pré saw the old Grange Hall ahead. White clapboard, a little building, smaller even than a schoolhouse. Some schoolhouses.

Du Pré glanced left and right. He saw Benny's four-wheel drive pickup off on some benchland a half mile or so away from the road. Du Pré slowed down. He saw a pair of ruts that went down into the barrow pit and up the other side and into the scrub. The ruts had been driven in recently.

Du Pré turned and the heavy police cruiser wallowed down and up and then he floored it. He kept an eye on the center of the tracks, looking for boulders, but this wasn't that kind of country. The rocks were up higher.

Then he hit one and he felt the transmission heave.

"Shit!" he snarled. He slowed down. The transmission whined. He smelled hot coolant.

Fuck me, Du Pré thought. Fuck me to death. Damn.

Benny Klein was sitting on the tailgate of his pickup. Du Pré parked the cruiser and he got out and walked to the sheriff. Benny was white and he was sweating even though the day was not warm.

"OK," said Du Pré.

"Over there," said Benny. He pointed toward some silvered boards piled haphazardly and clotted with the yellow skeletons of weeds from the last year.

An old lambing shed, maybe, who knew?

Du Pré walked slowly toward the pile of wood. A magpie floated past, headed for the creek a mile away.

Du Pré smelled the rotten flesh. Dead people, they smell deader than anything else. You smell a real dead person, you are smelling yourself someday, you never forget it.

She was lying facedown on a patch of yellow earth. The coyotes had eaten parts of her. Her legs were chewed. She was naked. She was swollen and greenish brown.

Du Pré squatted down on his haunches. He rolled a cigarette. He lit it with the rope shepherd's lighter his daughter Jacqueline had sent him from Spain, when she and her Raymond had gone there for a vacation.

Left me with all them babies, Du Pré thought, Madelaine not help me, Madelaine's daughters, I die.

Fourteen kids they got now. I don't think she is through yet.

Jesus.

Du Pré watched some maggots writhing under the dead girl's skin.

A gold chain glittered on her left ankle.

She had been blond.

Du Pré stood up and he walked around the body, a circle about six feet away. He brought the ground to his eyes, like he was tracking. He saw bombardier beetles struggling through the grass. Some tiny shards of green glass shone against the ocher earth.

Couple paper towels, slumped against a sagebrush. Been here a while. Yellow stains on them.

Du Pré circled out another two feet. The sagebrush was sparse here and clumps of grama grass spotted the harsh earth.

Rusty piece of barbwire, sticking out of the earth.

Du Pré ground his cigarette out under his bootheel.

He circled.

He stopped the fourth time he'd walked slowly around, counter-clockwise.

He looked back at the road.

He rolled another cigarette and he walked back to Benny, still sitting on the tailgate of the truck.

"Who finds her?" said Du Pré.

"One of the Salyer kids," said Benny. "Hunting gophers."

That kid not going to sleep so good, next month of nights.

"Your dispatcher, she call the State?"

Du Pré detested the dispatcher, who was a stupid bitch.

"Yeah," said Benny. "They're on their way. Probably be here, an hour. Said not to disturb anything."

Du Pré snorted. Same old shit.

"This not good," he said.

"No," said Benny. "It ain't. This animal is doing this, dumping the bodies. I just thought, shit, I bet there's a lot more. A lot more."

Du Pré sighed.

He glanced over toward a movement just out of his line of vision. A magpie had flown up from the sagebrush a couple hundred yards away.

"We never had anything like this before," said Benny.

Du Pré nodded.

A white pickup roared past on the road. The driver waved. Du Pré and Benny waved back.

In the night, Du Pré thought, a man could drive here, cut his lights, carry the bodies here in maybe ten, fifteen minutes, drive away, not turn his lights on till he was back on the highway. Have to have a lot of gas, couldn't afford to be seen buying any.

Benny's radio began to squawk.

Benny stood up and walked around to his cab and reached in and got the microphone. He listened for a while.

"Of course I'll stay here," he said, angrily. "What the hell do you think I am gonna do? Go play cards?"

"Well," the dispatcher's whiny voice said, "they asked me to call you."

"We actually wipe our butts and everything here, Iris," said Benny. "Those bastards are not going to be pleasant to have around."

"I was just trying to do my job . . ." whined Iris.

"OK, OK," said Benny. He clicked the microphone off.

"Poor Iris," said Benny. "Husband up and left, she's got six kids and two of them got in trouble and sent to Pine Hills."

Du Pré looked at Benny.

"Me," he said, "I don't be surprised her husband left, her kids are in jail. She is . . ."

"I know," said Benny.

Du Pré shrugged.

Benny walked morosely back to the tailgate and he sat down.

"Could I have a smoke?" said Benny.

Du Pré rolled him one.

"I don't need this shit," said Benny.

Du Pré nodded. It is your shit, though, Benny, you are the sheriff.

"That poor girl."

Du Pré stretched. He glanced off to his left.

Another magpie, same place.

Shit.

"OK," said Du Pré. "I think there is another one over there, so, Benny, why don't you just sit here, smoke."

"Oh, God," said Benny.

Du Pré got up and he started off toward the dark smear of sage that ran across his vision, there must be a slab of rock under it that caught water and held it.

Another magpie.

Shit.

Du Pré kept glancing down at the ground at his feet.

He was moving fast now, dancing through the sagebrush.

Du Pré heard drums in his head.

He smelled the smell of dead people, dead long enough to rot.

9

Du Pré looked hard.

He saw them then.

Two of them.

Du Pré looked hard and he drifted to his right, circling.

Two bodies, naked, laid out one atop the other, crossed.

Du Pré closed in. He rolled a smoke and lit it, to cut the smell.

He wished he'd brought a bottle with him from his car.

A sudden whiff of skunk. Du Pré saw the black-and-white creature waddling away.

These were awfully small women. Girls, really.

They had both been blond. The magpies and the scavengers had been at their faces. Flies buzzed around the eyepits. Their bellies were hugely swollen and the skin glazed with dirt.

These were fresher than the other, Du Pré thought, few days old.

Du Pré stopped.

He spat on the ground.

He moved away and he began to circle.

Him, Du Pré thought, he maybe leave more here.

Him, he like this place.

Why?

❖ CHAPTER 3 ❖

Right here," said Susan Klein. She was pale and angry. She shook her head. She rubbed the bartop with a towel.

The Toussaint Saloon was packed with people who were all talking at once in little groups. They were drinking but not much. They ordered drinks and then forgot them. The telephone was tied up with people who were checking on their families and friends. They did this over and over.

"It's something that happens somewhere else," said Susan Klein. "In the cities. It doesn't happen here."

Madelaine reached across the bar and she put her hand on top of Susan's. Madelaine looked down at the scarred wood.

Bart Fascelli was sucking down his second soda. His left arm was in a sling. Once again, he had hurt himself working on his gigantic diesel shovel. It did not come naturally to him.

"Bad man like that don't leave those girls nothin'," said Madelaine. "Kill them, dump them like old guts in the brush for the coyotes to eat."

Du Pré was standing on the other side of Bart, sipping a whiskey. He kept looking off somewhere else. Far away. A far country.

"I don't suppose it would do any good to post a reward?" said Bart, looking from Susan and Madelaine to Du Pré. Bart was rich. Very rich. He had money, at least, to offer.

Du Pré shrugged.

"I didn't think so," said Bart.

"It is maybe a good idea," said Du Pré. "Except this guy is not a thief or a guy does things with other people, you know. He just does this alone, you know. People now will be watching all the time, you bet, I hope they don't just shoot every stranger. This is not funny."

Benny Klein came in, looking tired and worn and sick.

He came up to his wife and he leaned up against the bar. He didn't say anything. After a moment, Susan reached over and touched his face.

"Benny," she said softly, "calm down. Have a beer. Come on, now."

Du Pré looked in the mirror. The four of them, the two women near poor Benny, who liked evil even less than he liked violence. Bart looking off and far away.

I hope he don't say he is afraid of me again, Du Pré thought. I hope this bastard gets caught today. But I don't think that he will.

Du Pré's thoughts flicked back and forth like a hunter's eyes on a landscape. He sighed and sipped his whiskey.

Susan Klein was pulling beers and mixing drinks, her face sad.

I been here plenty, thought Du Pré, playing my fiddle. Happy times with my friends and neighbors, drinking and laughing and dancing. Maybe we get to do that. But we have to wait on someone with a dead heart to let us.

"Gabriel," said Bart. He had come up behind Du Pré.

"Unh," said Du Pré.

"What do you think, now?" said Bart. He was looking levelly into Du Pré's eyes.

Du Pré shrugged.

He rolled a cigarette. He lit it.

"Plenty bad, what I think," said Du Pré. "Maybe I call that Harvey Wallace, you remember?"

"Oh, yes," said Bart.

"He is with them FBI," Du Pré went on. "Maybe he have something he can tell us."

"Good," said Bart.

"I also try to find Benetsee," said Du Pré. "But he is gone. He tell me he is going to Canada, see some of his people. But I don't know what he meant, how long he is gone, you know."

"I'm trying to think of something I can do," said Bart.

"You are doing it," said Du Pré. "You can spend your money later."

Bart laughed.

"It's the first thing that I think of," he said, "you know how I am."

Du Pré looked up at the tin ceiling. Yes, Bart, I know how you are and you got more money than most countries got. It almost killed you, all that money. But it did not.

You are my friend.

My father kill your brother, long time ago.

Life, it is very strange.

Du Pré stubbed his smoke out in the ashtray. Light flashed against the ceiling, someone had opened the door.

Clouds moved, Du Pré thought. He glanced over to see who had come in.

A middle-aged couple in new heavy jackets and the sort of shoes

12

that city people buy to go to the country in were standing inside the door, and they looked uncomfortable.

The man took the woman's arm and led her toward the bar, he bent over and was speaking softly close to her ear. She looked at the floor and she dabbed at her eyes with a handkerchief.

Susan Klein had seen the couple and she had come out from the bar, moving very quickly.

Du Pré looked at her, standing in front of them, her face grave.

They talked in low tones. Susan glanced over at Du Pré.

She said one more thing to them and then she led them over to where Du Pré was sitting. Du Pré got up.

"This is Mr. and Mrs. Kamp," said Susan Klein to Du Pré. "They are the parents . . . of a missing girl. They wanted to talk . . . to you . . ."

Missing girl, Du Pré thought. Oh, yes, they are missing, they just up and left for hell.

The woman looked up at Du Pré. She was a tiny creature, her eyes huge in her sad face.

"Shannon was . . ." she began.

"Our daughter," the man cut in. "She ran away a year ago . . . we never heard from her again."

"We just want to know . . ." the woman said.

Du Pré nodded. "The police, they call you?"

"No," said the man. "They haven't . . . they said they haven't been able to identify any of the victims . . ."

The woman had pulled a photograph from the pocket of her coat. It was an ordinary yearbook photograph, the kind kids in high school pass around.

"She looked like this," said the woman. "Isn't she pretty?"

Du Pré took the photograph. He stared at it.

If one of them was your daughter, I would not know it, he thought, their faces had been chewed almost off, they had rotted, there was nothing there that looked like a pretty girl, like this picture.

"The police won't let us look at the bodies," said the woman.

No shit, thought Du Pré, you look at what we are finding out there you will not sleep again, this lifetime.

"She was so pretty . . ." the woman said, again.

"Could you tell us anything?" said the man. "She had a birthmark on her back."

Du Pré thought of the green-brown bloated mess lying in the sagebrush, the birds pecking at it.

"I don't know," said Du Pré, lamely. "I wish I could help, you know, but you will have to wait for the police."

"But you found them," said the man. He was getting angry.

Du Pré nodded.

"Why can't you tell us about Shannon?" said the woman.

Du Pré felt his temper rise. Then it cooled. Crazy question, these are people crazy with grief, he thought, they are mad.

"It's a conspiracy," said the man.

Yes, Du Pré thought, it is.

"Do you know what it is like, to lose a child and not even really know what happened to her?" said the woman.

Du Pré nodded.

"Why won't you help us?" said the man.

"He is helping you," said Susan Klein.

"Bastards," said the woman.

Susan narrowed her eyes. She stalked out the front door of the bar. She was gone only a couple of minutes. When she came back, she had a manila envelope in her hand.

"Oh, God, Susan," said Benny.

"My husband is trying to find this animal," said Susan Klein to the couple. "So is Gabriel, and about five hundred other cops. Cops are people. Pretty good people."

She pulled a big glossy black-and-white photo from the envelope.

"Is this your daughter?" said Susan, eyes blazing.

The couple looked at the photo.

"What is it?" said the woman.

"It's what Gabriel found," said Susan. "They don't look like what you see in a funeral parlor when the cops find them. They look like this."

"Oh my God," said the man. "That's a body."

"People aren't good keepers," said Susan Klein.

"I don't understand," said the woman.

"Good," said Susan Klein, slipping the photo back in the envelope. "Now, mister, I suggest that you take your wife and get the hell out of my bar and don't come back for a while."

"Why?" said the woman.

"Come on, Grace," said the man, pulling on his wife's arm.

She went with him, shaking her head.

They went out.

Susan Klein went back behind the bar.

Du Pré looked at her.

She was lighting a cigarette with a butane lighter.

It took her four tries. Her hands were shaking. Badly.

✤ CHAPTER 4 ✤

They have to do it that way," said Harvey Wallace, whose Indian name was Weasel Fat. He was Blackfeet, and FBI.

"Shit," said Du Pré. "It was some surprising, you know, they come here and they want to question me, you know. Then this guy of yours, he says, Mr. Du Pré, we know you are killing these girls, we want to *help* you."

"Yeah," said Harvey Wallace/Weasel Fat. "Well, that is the way that they do things."

"They ever *catch* anybody," said Du Pré into the telephone. He was so mad he was shouting.

"Fairly often," said Harvey. "We catch bad guys pretty often. You'd be surprised. I know I look like a dickhead, but even I have caught bad guys. Jury even agreed."

"I am sorry," said Du Pré. "I am pret' mad, say things."

"Don't blame you," said Harvey, "now, he'll probably come on back and want you to take a polygraph."

"Lie detector?" said Du Pré. "Jesus Christ."

"Yeah," said Harvey. "Please take it."

"Why the fuck I take *that?*" said Du Pré.

"Well," said Harvey. "If you pass it, then you're out of it altogether."

"Harvey," said Du Pré, "I am out of it now."

"No," said Harvey. "You aren't. Tell you a story. Ten years ago, we had a case, guy was killing little girls, you know, like five years old. Cops are stumped. We come in. We don't get squat. Couple more little girls get found. There's no thread."

Du Pré rolled a cigarette with one hand. He'd taken two years off when he was sixteen and he had done nothing much but try to roll cigarettes with one hand. Like his Papa, Catfoot, did. Got so he could do it pretty good. Two years.

"I come in on it and I look over all the reports. Nothin'. I can't see anything. Case drags on a year. Three more little girls. The people in this city are ready to lynch all the incompetent bastards in the FBI."

Du Pré struck a match with his thumbnail. Some of the match's phosphorous stuck under his thumbnail, burning. It hurt like hell. Du Pré glared at the pain.

"I can't see a fucking thing. Hundreds of leads followed, a few suspects but nothing worth spit, they all got good alibis, nothing, not one fucking thing. So I send all the reports to Statistical Analysis. They put the data into the computer. The computer notices that there is this one cop who is around more than he should be, it's not his case but he's around it a lot."

"You give him the pollywog, whatever," said Du Pré, "And it's him?"

"Not quite," said Harvey. "I have him take the polygraph and he's lying about something. But he didn't kill the little girls. Polygraph says so, so does a bunch of other things."

Du Pré sucked on his burnt thumb.

"I am curious," said Harvey. "So I grill this poor bastard over a nice hot flame, woulda put burning toothpicks under his fingernails, skinned him slowly, it is the way of my people."

Them Blackfeet, mean fuckers, thought Du Pré, looking at his thumb.

"Well," said Harvey, "after working his kidneys over with a rubber hose and threatening to fry up his pet guppies for lunch, he finally breaks and tells me about the report he didn't file. Seems he was working and a call got routed to him, the dicks on the case were all out. Some little old lady had seen something suspicious. Ho-hum, little old ladies drive us nuts."

Du Pré clenched his teeth. His thumb hurt like hell.

"Well, this poor cop was going through a bad divorce and he'd gobbled too many Valiums and he was kinda addled, and he scrambled everything he jotted down and then he went home and slept it off and when he came back the next day he couldn't make fuck-all out of his notes so he trashed them."

Du Pré farted.

"Case goes on, the cop is obsessed with this little old lady who called in when he was all fucked up, but he can't find her. It's the one time he's ever done this. He's ashamed. The little old lady had given him the license plate number of a car."

Du Pré waited.

"Finally I say, look, here's what you do. Go back and work out from the places where the little girls were found. See if any little old ladies croaked after the day you were too fucked up to take the call."

"By midafternoon the cop's got a name of an old lady who stroked out three days after one of the bodies was discovered. He goes to look at the house. House has a clear view though it's pretty far off. Goes up to the house. It's sealed, pending probate. He gets a court order and gets in. What do you think he finds?"

"This old lady," said Du Pré, "she has this telescope, she looks out the window with. She writes things down. There is a note by the telephone, got description of a guy, a car, the license plate number, the time, and everything."

"Exactly," said Harvey. "How'd you guess that?"

"I never heard you speak more than fifty words at once, all the time I know you," said Du Pré. "So I figure it has to be a real story and so that is how a real story would work out."

"Indeed it did," said Harvey. "Picked the guy up, grilled him, sent in Come-to-Jesus Wilkins, and the guy confessed just like that."

"Come-to-Jesus?" said Du Pré.

"FBI agent who, so help me, can go into a room with a raving sociopath and convince the motherfucker that he ought to do the best thing. Come-to-Jesus, get it off his chest and straight with the Lord. I saw him do it once with a wacko who ate everyone he killed."

Du Pré snorted.

"So," said Harvey Wallace/Weasel Fat, "I'd appreciate it if as a personal favor to me you would take the polygraph."

"Fuck," said Du Pré.

"Fine," said Harvey. "Just after you take the polygraph. Now, after you take the polygraph I can be more helpful than I can before."

"Shit," said Du Pré.

"Du Pré," said Harvey, "humor me. This is almost the twenty-first century and gadgets rule us."

"You think I maybe done this?" said Du Pré.

"Don't be an asshole," said Harvey. "Of course not. But once you take it then all the guys in the agency who live and die by the damn things are stalemated and they cause less trouble. I won't be assigned to that case. Wish I could be. I keep telling them they are fools and they keep promoting me."

"OK," said Du Pré. "You gonna have Benny take it? He is so upset he probably flunk it."

"You don't worry about that," said Harvey. "Benny's the Sheriff and he's not the problem. You are. You have no official status."

18

"Oh," said Du Pré.

"Which means I can't talk to you much," said Harvey.

"I am going, this murderer, I am going to find him," said Du Pré.

"Probably," said Harvey. "Benny won't. You might."

"OK," said Du Pré, "I get him to deputize me?"

"Yup," said Harvey.

"Then what?" said Du Pré.

"I send Agent Pidgeon to see you."

"Why?" said Du Pré.

"She's a specialist in serial killers," said Harvey.

"She?" said Du Pré.

"Yeah," said Harvey. "We quit binding their feet, taught 'em how to read, write, things like that. Nothing to be done about it now, we got 'em."

"How long she been doing this?" said Du Pré.

"Couple years," said Harvey. "She got her doctorate in psychology and then she joined the FBI. Nice young woman. Beautiful, too. Ambitious. Great knockers. Smart. If she heard me tell you she had great knockers, I'd be jailed for sexual harassment. Lose my job."

"Why she pick serial killers?" said Du Pré.

"You'd have to ask her," said Harvey. "I'd be afraid to, myself."

"OK," said Du Pré. "I go to this polygraph."

"It makes things simpler," said Harvey.

"Who do I call?" said Du Pré.

"Oh," said Harvey, "I already did."

"Prick," said Du Pré. "You know I say yes, huh?"

"Yup," said Harvey. "I need you on this one, we do anyway."

"OK," said Du Pré.

"Bodies are dumped out in the sagebrush," said Harvey. "Very few FBI guys know much about sagebrush."

"Yah," said Du Pré. "I am trying to find Benetsee."

"That would have been my next question," said Harvey.

"He is in Canada," said Du Pré.

19

"I'll send you some money," said Harvey. "You buy him some wine and tobacco and meat."

"Oh," said Du Pré, "I take care of it."

"Thanks," said Harvey.

"Yeah," said Du Pré.

✤ CHAPTER 5 ✤

"Du Pré!" said Madelaine. "You ask him to ask you them question I give you."

"Yah," said Du Pré. "He ask me I am fucking twelve women, like you keep telling me I am, I say no, the machine, it says I am lying."

"OK," said Madelaine. "I thought so."

"It is fourteen, anyway," said Du Pré. "My dick, it is huge and it is very hungry. Twelve women, they do not quite do it for me, you know."

"OK," said Madelaine. "I fix that. You don't be telling me, you have a headache, you hear."

Du Pré nodded and grinned at her.

"Now on, you don't got time, fuck more than me," said Madelaine.

"Love is holy," said Father Van Den Heuvel. "And never more so than when the two of you discuss it."

The three of them were sitting at Madelaine's kitchen table having lunch. Elk and vegetable soup and Madelaine's good bread and home-canned corn and peppers.

The big, clumsy Belgian Jesuit had splotches of elk soup and kernels of corn down his cassock.

Been a while since he knock himself out shutting his head in his car door, Du Pré thought, he should maybe do that pretty soon again.

Three times the good priest had been found lying by his car, out cold. He was the clumsiest human being Du Pré had ever known. He was not allowed to split wood anymore. He had split his own foot so badly he was two years on crutches.

It was maybe the only congregation in the world which laid bets on whether or not the priest would drop the Host during Communion.

There was half a foot of snow outside on the ground. Even though it was the first week of June, it was Montana, and it seemed to snow at least every other year in early June. Late June.

"It ever snow here in July?" said Father Van Den Heuvel. "I think it has snowed every other month."

"Yah," said Du Pré. "We got two feet once, Fourth of July."

"Ah," said Father Van Den Heuvel, "God's love is wonderful."

"It is sad, them girls, no one know who they are," said Madelaine.

Only one of the three bodies could be identified. Father Van Den Heuvel had buried the unknown two this morning. The county had paid for the coffins.

"Poor children," said the big priest. "I wonder where their families are."

"Lots of runaway kids," said Madelaine.

The pathologists had said that the two bodies that Du Pré had found were approximately sixteen. Dental work had been of minimal quality. One of the girls had a tattoo, the kind made in jails with pen inks and dull needles. A skull with a cross sticking out of it.

On the web of skin between thumb and forefinger of her left hand. The girl may have done it herself.

"How come they bury them so quick?" said Madelaine.

"They get their samples and that is that," said Du Pré.

Modern times.

Don't want to pay the cold storage on them, Du Pré thought. These are not kids from nice homes. People who have some power, money.

21

These kids, they will be forgotten. They always were forgotten. Their parents never even knew that they were there, I bet.

Only Du Pré and Madelaine and Benny had come to the interment. Benny left immediately.

Father Van Den Heuvel had said his few words and then he and Du Pré and Benny had let the coffins down. They were very light.

"Du Pré!" Madelaine said. "I want you to promise these two little girls that you will find who did this to them. They got no one else to speak for them, you know."

"Yah," said Du Pré.

"You promise them."

"They don't got names," said Du Pré, "so I say, OK, you are my people, I find this bastard."

Madelaine reached up and touched Du Pré on his cheek.

"Everybody is our people," said Madelaine. "We are Métis."

Du Pré nodded. That was true. The Mixed Bloods. That is pretty much everybody.

Long time ago, my people who were in France come to the New World and they marry my people who were already here. Then we really catch hell. Whites call us Indian, Indians call us whites. English, they hang us, steal our land. Send us all across Canada, move them furs for the Hudson's Bay Company. The Here Before Christ. Most places they were, too.

Long time ago.

They come down here after them English crush the Red River Rebellion, got nothing, bunches of children.

Had each other, my people did.

These poor girls, they have no one at all.

They got my Madelaine, who would feed all the world. Wipe all the tears.

They got me, too, I guess.

I find this bastard.

Du Pré rolled a cigarette while he waited for Father Van Den Heuvel to come back from taking a leak. The old police cruiser, light bar and sirens taken off, decals off the doors, still runs good. Runs fast.

There were a lot of cigarette burns on the backseat, where smokes Du Pré had flicked out the window flew back in.

Du Pré rolled a cigarette and he offered it to Father Van Den Heuvel. The big priest nodded and he took it. He had never tried to roll his own smoke. He couldn't do it.

"I must go," said the big priest. "I have to drive to Miles City and see Mrs. LeBlanc. She is dying."

"I send her something?" said Madelaine.

"She can't eat," said Father Van Den Heuvel.

Madelaine dug around and she found a St. Christopher medal.

Father Van Den Heuvel put it in his pocket.

Madelaine walked him out to his car. Du Pré had some more coffee.

Tomorrow, I got to go sign off, some cattle. His son-in-law, Raymond, did most of the brand inspections now, but Du Pré did what Raymond could not do. Cattle business was not too good. Hate someone, give them a cow. Cattle business was mostly not too good.

Du Pré heard the priest's car drive off. Madelaine came back.

"You sure like, devil that poor priest," said Du Pré.

"Poo," said Madelaine. "Him like it. He is a nice man."

Du Pré laughed.

"Devil me, too," he said.

Madelaine stood in front of him, hand on her hip.

"Fourteen, huh?" she said. "You come on now, I show you some damn fourteen."

After, Du Pré sat on the edge of the bed, smoking. Madelaine was in the shower. Du Pré could smell the potpourri soap she made, the smell of the steam from the hot water. The door to the bathroom was open and he could see her shape through the glass door of the shower.

Fourteen, huh? Du Pré thought, I got as much trouble I need, just this Madelaine. She fuck good. I am a lucky man.

Where is old Benetsee? My old coyote friend. Him, he got things to tell me that I need to hear.

Who is, this man does these things. What does he hide behind? Where is he going? I want to kill him, where do I wait.

Thing about good hunters, they wait well. Don't bother them, they dream, don't move.

When Madelaine came out of the bathroom in her robe, toweling her thick long dark hair, Du Pré went in and he showered quickly. He dried himself and he got dressed and he went out to the kitchen.

"I am going to Benetsee's," he said.

Madelaine nodded. "Him not back."

Du Pré shrugged.

"Leave him a note," said Madelaine.

"Don't know, him read," said Du Pré.

"Then you leave him note he don't have to read," said Madelaine. "You leave him a loaf of my good bread."

She went to the kitchen and she wrapped up a loaf of bread in foil and she put it in a plastic bag.

"His dogs all dead?" she said.

Du Pré nodded. Dogs got old, they died.

"We get him another dog," said Madelaine.

"OK," said Du Pré. He did not ever argue with Madelaine. She had taught him not to do that.

"Old man," said Madelaine. "I pray for him."

"You pray for everybody," said Du Pré.

"Don't pray for your fourteen other women," said Madelaine.

"Them don't need it," said Du Pré.

"I find you, another woman, you need it," said Madelaine.

"OK," said Du Pré.

"You find that man," said Madelaine.

✤ CHAPTER 6 ✤

Du Pré and Madelaine watched the fancydancers circling on the floor of the high-school gymnasium. Men with huge feather bustles and fans and headdresses and legpieces and all of them as proud as fighting cocks. Fancydancers. Roosters.

Wolf Point, Montana. It felt cold here even if it was hot.

"Let's go, look at the things the traders have," said Madelaine. There were tables and booths all up and down the halls of the schools. Jewelry, clothing, crafts, one man even had some buffalo robes.

They walked down the steps of the bleachers and out into the lobby. Madelaine looked around at the displays of junk jewelry, most of it bad turquoise and cheap silverplate, made in Southeast Asia.

She spotted an old man in a ribbon shirt who didn't have very much. Just a black cloth, worn velvet, sprawled on a card table and a few pieces set on it. The old man stood with his arms folded. He had big rings on each finger and thumb and bracelets and a necklace of silver rattlesnakes with turquoise eyes.

Madelaine stopped in front of the table.

"How far are you from your people?" she said.

"Long ways," said the man. He smiled. He had no front teeth.

Madelaine bent over to look. She picked up a bracelet which had a huge cabochon of black-spotted turquoise set in a mass of silver. She turned the bracelet around. She squinted at the back of the setting.

"I like this," she said. "Will you sell it?"

"Thousand dollars," said the old man.

Madelaine nodded.

"He say a thousand dollars."

"He does, eh?" said Du Pré, who hated shopping.

Madelaine smiled at him.

"You trade this for a good fiddle?" she said.

"Mebbe," said the old man. "If I can play it as well as your man the first time I pick it up."

Du Pré snorted.

"Five hundred," said Madelaine.

"OK," said the old man, smiling. "I give this to you, five hundred and half his fiddle. I got a saw in my truck."

Du Pré nodded. He wondered if he had seven hundred dollars on him, since that was where Madelaine and this toothless old man were headed, after they had got through threatening to saw Du Pré's fiddle in half. He probably did.

They stood there for a moment. A band of teenage Indian kids ran past laughing. They all had on black satin jackets with red feather fans on the backs. They were headed outside to smoke.

Inside the drummers and singers were making music. The sound was very old and eerie. It had been going on here in America for thousands of years. Du Pré looked through the open doors and he saw the fancydancers speeding up, through the crowd of people drifting past. Sometimes the fancydancers danced for hours. Some dropped dead of heart attacks. It was an exhausting dance.

"Seven hundred dollars," said Madelaine.

Du Pré dug out his wallet. He looked in one of the side pockets where he kept his hundred-dollar bills. There were two wads in it. He usually only carried one. He fished out the wad, quartered, that didn't look familiar. There were seven hundred-dollar bills in it. He handed them to Madelaine.

The old man was fitting the bracelet to Madelaine's wrist, squeezing the soft silver with his strong old hands.

Du Pré handed him the money. The old man didn't count it, he just tucked it in his shirt pocket.

Du Pré looked back at the fancydancers. They were rocking back and forth as they circled, dipping forward and arching their backs.

Du Pré ached looking at them.

The drums went faster, the singers ululated.

"Thanks, Du Pré," said Madelaine.

"Uh," said Du Pré. "There is this seven hundred dollars there I don't know I got."

"Oh, how is that?" said Madelaine. "One of your women you fucking tip you, you were so good one night?"

"No," said Du Pré. "One I am fucking put it in my wallet, though."

"Well," said Madelaine. "Maybe, who knows."

Du Pré laughed.

There was food being served in the cafeteria. They went in. There were pots of buffalo stew and fry bread and chokecherry syrup. Cost two dollars. They took their food to a table and Du Pré went to buy some soft drinks.

"They don't got pink wine," said Du Pré, setting down the paper cups.

"No shit they don't," said Madelaine. "They don't allow no alcohol at all here. Too much trouble."

"I got whiskey in my truck," said Du Pré.

"They find it they beat the shit out of you," said Madelaine.

Some of the young men, who were the security people, came in, and they looked pretty tough.

"Probably," said Du Pré.

"Well," said Madelaine. "There are some of your Turtle Mountain people."

Du Pré glanced over. He waved at the Turtle Mountain people, in their bright red shirts and cowboy hats and boots.

"We play some tonight," said Du Pré.

It started to rain outside, sudden slashing rain with a lot of wind. The sheet of glass in the windows flexed and shimmered.

The buffalo stew didn't have enough salt in it. Du Pré got up and he went to get some.

He found some little packets of salt. He took ten.

He went back. Madelaine was looking at her new bracelet.

"It is very pretty," he said.

"Yes," said Madelaine. "Me, I like this."

They ate their food. Pretty bland. Du Pré wished he had some pepper sauce.

"You want to smoke," said Madelaine, "you will have to go outside. Me, I will go and look around, these other traders."

Du Pré laughed.

"You want money?" he said.

Madelaine shook her head. "I got my nice thing," she said. "You go and smoke."

Du Pré carried the used bowls and plates and plastic forks to a trash can and he dumped them in. Madelaine grinned at him and she went off down a side hall rowed both sides with tables.

Du Pré made his way out front. The sidewalk was thick with cigarette butts.

The rain had stopped as suddenly as it had begun. The sun was shining down in golden shafts through the black clouds. The air was fresh and smelled of lightning.

Du Pré rolled a cigarette and he lit it and he drew the smoke deep into his lungs. He blew out a long blue-gray stream. He sighed. It tasted good.

Knots of people stood around, smoking and chatting. Little kids shrieked and ran and jumped. Their parents were inside, shrieking and running and jumping, some of them anyway.

Young bloods in ribbon shirts with fancy hairdos announced their tribe by their clothes and paints and bad attitudes of young warriors.

Du Pré snorted. Backbone of the tribe is the women, they give life, strength of the tribe is the warriors, their humility.

These boys, they got some to go, Du Pré thought. Spend a little less time, front of the mirror, little more time helping the old people.

Du Pré glanced off at a little copse of blue spruce in the middle of the lawn. There was a sculpture made of stainless steel to one side.

An old man dressed in ragged clothes was leaning against the sculpture.

It was Benetsee.

"Damn," said Du Pré. He threw his cigarette on the ground and he began to walk toward the old man.

"Hey!" Du Pré yelled.

Benetsee moved. He was shuffling, fast enough, toward the little stand of spruces.

Du Pré got to the lawn and he started to run.

Benetsee went behind the trees.

Du Pré cursed.

He ran flat out, his cowboy boots slipping at each stride with a jerk, leather soles on wet grass.

Du Pré tried to turn and his feet shot out from under him and he fell full-length.

He slid a good fifteen feet. He was all wet on his right side. He could smell the crushed grass. His jeans would be stained. The elbow of his shirt.

Du Pré got up and he walked on, his side stitched a little, he had pulled some muscles in his chest.

Du Pré went around behind the spruces.

No one there. Of course.

Du Pré heard feet running toward him.

A couple of the young security men came around the spruces, one on each side.

"Hey, man," said one. "Everything all right? We saw you running."

"Oh, yes," said Du Pré. "It is all right."

The three of them looked at each other for a moment.

Du Pré shrugged and he walked back toward the gym.

✤ CHAPTER 7 ✤

Them powwows all the same," said Madelaine. "Same people doin' same things. I go to 'em, but I don't miss leavin' them." Madelaine grinned at Du Pré. She had her left hand on the dashboard of the car. The turquoise bracelet burned sea blue in the sunlight.

Du Pré glanced over at the fence line crossing a little feeder seep. A prairie falcon gripped a post, wings half-extended.

They were doing about eighty on a narrow two-lane blacktop road. Every once in a while, they passed a little white cross mounted on a steel fencepost. The crosses marked spots where people had died in car wrecks. On Memorial Day, family would often put plastic flowers on the crosses.

"I had some good times with them Turtle Mountain people," said Du Pré. "Them good people."

"That guitar player, him Daby, is a dirty old man," said Madelaine. "He grab my ass, you know."

"Um," said Du Pré. Well, he thought, you can eat old Daby for your lunch, the old bastard won't try that again, I am sure. Maybe he drive, Turtle Mountain, ice bag in his lap, keep the hurt from his nuts getting ripped off down a little.

"He play pretty good guitar, though," Madelaine said.

She don't rip his nuts off. She tell him, you play pretty good, I don't rip your plums off this one time, you know. Second time, I take 'em, fry them, eat them. Turtle Mountain oysters.

"I tell him, mind your manners, I fry up some Turtle Mountain oysters." said Madelaine. "Him don't like that."

They crested a long sloping hill and looked down suddenly into a swaled bottom, thick with cattails and loud with Canada geese. The car windows were shut but the geese honked loudly enough so they could be heard easily. Du Pré glanced over and saw young geese, in their yellow down, following their parents.

The car bottomed out as it crossed a little bridge and then shot up the rising road. A pheasant flew suddenly.

Above the water's reach to the roots hanging down into the earth, the sagebrush reappeared.

They got to Toussaint in two hours. It was a bright and sunny day and the Wolf Mountains to the north gleamed with fresh snow up high.

"You want some pink wine?" said Du Pré.

"No," said Madelaine. "I need to go home. I am a little worried about Lourdes."

Lourdes was Madelaine's eldest daughter. A good student, quiet and shy, when she grew up she would be a stately woman. She had her father's big bones and blade nose.

Du Pré nodded. Lourdes had just turned fifteen and she was the most rebellious of Madelaine's children, in a quiet, firm way. No scenes. No calls from the police. If she drank or smoked dope she did so very quietly. Du Pré didn't think that she did.

Lourdes liked to control everything around her.

Lourdes was a frightened, intelligent girl.

Du Pré drove up to Madelaine's house. The front door was open. The radio was turned up very loud. Bad rock and roll music.

It was all pretty bad, Du Pré thought.

Du Pré parked and he got out and opened the trunk and he got their nylon suitcases. He took one in each hand and he walked up toward the house.

"Du Pré!" Madelaine yelled. Her voice was a little hysterical.

Du Pré came in. He set the bags down.

Madelaine was standing by the telephone, which sat on a little Parsons table Du Pré had made for her, out of some walnut he had found in an abandoned bar.

Madelaine was holding a piece of ruled notebook paper. The sort that is bound with wire. One margin was all tiny holes, now ripped out when the page had been taken from the book.

"Lourdes, she run away."

Du Pré nodded. Neither of his two girls had ever run away, but, then, neither of his two girls got any crap from Du Pré, who knew better. My Jacqueline and my Maria, they know who they are. Father Pussycat, they call me. I give up early on.

"She say where she run away to?" said Du Pré.

"It is not running away you let your poor mother know where you are visiting," said Madelaine. "That's just visiting."

"She got a boyfriend?" said Du Pré.

"Yeah," said Madelaine. "She is hanging out with that poor Das-

31

sault boy, Sean. That asshole old man of his, name him that."

Bucky Dassault was one of Du Pré's pet hates. The man was wholly dishonest. He'd come out of Deer Lodge Prison on parole from a statutory rape conviction. While he was in there, he had taken extension courses and qualified as an alcohol and drug counselor. That didn't work out well, so he became Benjamin Medicine Eagle, New Age Shaman, and he took out ads in New Age magazines and he made a lot of money. His wife had the good sense to divorce him after only three kids. Sean was around, but the other boy and the girl were in juvenile custodial programs.

"So we ask Sean, where is Lourdes?" said Du Pré.

"No shit," said Madelaine.

"OK," said Du Pré. "I go and find the little prick and talk with him, you maybe make some phone calls."

"You don't hurt him," said Madelaine. "He's a pretty good kid, don't have much at home, you know. You can scare him some, but you don't hurt him, Du Pré."

Du Pré nodded. He wasn't going to hurt poor Sean in the first place, but then Madelaine mothered even people she hated.

Du Pré went out and he got in the car and he drove down to the bar and he got out and he went in.

Susan Klein was standing behind the bar. Her husband Benny was out in front.

Sean Dassault was sitting on a barstool, cringing.

"She mad about something," he whined. He turned and looked and saw Du Pré and he jumped off the stool and tried to run.

Benny Klein held his arm.

"You want to kill him or can I?" said Benny.

"OOhhhhh," wailed Sean.

"Sean," said Du Pré, "you quit bawling, some stuck pig, there. We are worried about Lourdes."

Sean looked at Du Pré warily.

"She pregnant?" said Du Pré.

Sean turned red and shook his head.

Bingo, thought Du Pré. Little bastards act just like we did. Now we know better, spoil their fun.

"You know where she go?"

"She was going to Seattle," said Sean.

"How is she getting, this Seattle, Sean?" said Du Pré.

"She going to hitchhike," said Sean.

"Where from?" said Du Pré.

"Going up to the Hi-Line," said Sean.

"Who give her a ride there?" said Du Pré. "Or . . . wait a minute, she was running, the track meet in Cut Bank?"

"She don't go, she tell them she is sick, first thing on Saturday morning."

Me and Madelaine, we are at the powwow. Smart kid.

"Who give her the ride there?" said Du Pré.

"I did," Sean sniffled.

Oh, good, thought Du Pré, Lourdes has the balls to hitchhike a thousand miles, and you, you little pile of shit, won't go along to protect her. Not that you could so much, but the thought is nice.

"Why don't you go?" said Du Pré.

"I am eighteen," said Sean miserably.

Right, thought Du Pré, that is statutory rape, even if you don't touch them, here. OK, this kid is at least not wanting to see Deer Lodge first minute he is eligible, go there.

"You try to talk her out of it?"

"Hah," said Sean. "She don't never do what I say."

"You take her yesterday morning?" said Du Pré.

Sean nodded.

"Drop her off, Raster Creek, first place got a little rest stop?"

Sean nodded.

"You wait to see, she gets a ride?"

Sean shook his head.

"Why not?" said Du Pré.

"She don't want me to," Sean said.

"We got girls dead in the sagebrush," said Du Pré, "and you, you little fucker, you don't at least wait, see who picks her up?"

Sean shook his head miserably.

"You pussy-whipped little bastard," said Du Pré. "Good thing I don't not promise my Madelaine that I won't hurt you."

"She tell me, go away," said Sean.

"Madelaine, she skin you out, whole hide," said Du Pré. "She wipe her ass with your brain. You want good advice, grow a foot, turn blond, move away. Jesus."

Sean snuffled.

"Sean," said Susan Klein, "you fucked up big time."

"Well," said Du Pré, "since you are gonna die so soon, you maybe better go find Father Van Den Heuvel."

"Oh," said Sean.

"It is important," said Du Pré.

"Oh," said Sean.

"Madelaine, she will not kill you while there is a priest looking," said Du Pré. "He quit looking at you, you dead."

Sean looked at Du Pré, and Susan, and Benny. He snuffled and wiped his nose on a bar napkin.

He went out the side door and headed for the little Catholic Church.

Du Pré rolled a smoke.

"Poor little fucker," he said.

✦ CHAPTER 8 ✦

God damn you Harvey Weasel Fat, I thought me and you were friends!" Madelaine said not very sweetly into the telephone.

Du Pré couldn't hear Harvey defend himself.

"You talkin' like a man got a velvet mouth," said Madelaine. "Why you don't help me?"

Harvey, he is not doing so good, thought Du Pré.

"I got a daughter out there bein' fucked by truck drivers if she isn't dead," said Madelaine. "You goddamn right I am upset. You bastards so busy burning down churches full of dumb people you got no time for a poor woman who's worried?"

She really is mad, thought Du Pré. Mothers, they go nuts, their kids give them mental illness.

"What you care some pussy white man give you a bunch of dumb rules?" said Madelaine. "You Indian or what?"

Poor Harvey, thought Du Pré, he forget it is the women in the tribe do all the torturing. Nothing they like better, saw off nuts with a dull rock.

"Well, I thank you," said Madelaine, "you skinny Blackfeet prick."

Madelaine slammed the phone down.

"Asshole," she said.

Du Pré went to her and he took her in his arms and she began to cry softly. She buried her head in his chest. She put her hands to her face and she rocked a little, keening.

"What I do wrong?" said Madelaine. "I love that Lourdes, I know she is not having such a good time, you know? What I do wrong?"

Du Pré had an attack of smarts and he didn't say one damn thing.

"Damn," said Madelaine. She sniffled. She pulled away and went to the roll of paper towels in the kitchen and she ripped one off and blew her nose and wiped her eyes. She went off to the bathroom. Du Pré heard the water running in the sink.

She will be better now, Du Pré thought, not OK but better.

That damn little bitch Lourdes. She got to know how worried this will make her mother.

Not to mention me. That guy, he is out there, eating runaways.

Dumping their poor bodies in the sagebrush.

That guy, he had a mother, too. We all get one.

Where is he?

Madelaine came out of the bathroom. Her eyes were swollen but a little clearer. Her black eyebrows were knotted and her hands were clenched tight.

"You call them Missoula police?" she said.

"Yes," said Du Pré. Also Kalispell, Spokane, Seattle.

This would be plenty bad enough without what else we got, Du Pré thought. She ought to be crazy.

There was a knock at the door. Du Pré went to it.

Father Van Den Heuvel and Bart.

Du Pré motioned them in.

"You want some coffee," said Madelaine, looking up at them. "I get you some. You sit."

They sat.

Madelaine put water on the stove and they heard the coffee grinder, a heavy cast-iron one maybe a hundred years old, crank.

"I have a plane here," said Bart.

Du Pré nodded. Sometimes it was good to have a rich friend.

"Not much to do but wait and pray," said Father Van Den Heuvel.

No shit, thought Du Pré.

The three men sat and waited, motionless and silent. Madelaine brought coffee for everybody and they drank it.

"How is that Sean?" said Madelaine suddenly.

She looked at Father Van Den Heuvel.

"Upset," said the big priest. "He doesn't feel he did the right thing."

"Where he is?" said Madelaine.

"Uh," said the priest. "He's . . ."

"He's hidin' out at your place," said Madelaine. "I better go and see him. Poor little guy. My Lourdes wrap him around his own dick just like that. Him, he is not match for her, for sure. It is not his fault. I better go tell him that."

Du Pré looked away and smiled.

"I'll go and get him," said Bart.

"I will go with you," said Madelaine. "I . . . you two stay here, you answer the phone."

Du Pré and Father Van Den Heuvel nodded.

Madelaine grabbed her purse and she and Bart went out.

"It's terrible," said the priest. "Poor Madelaine. Poor Lourdes."

"She is a good girl," said Du Pré. "Just strong-willed like her mother. She be all right."

They sat.

Du Pré heard the grind of a big truck moving from a stop up to a slow speed.

It was coming around the corner of the main street and heading up toward Madelaine's.

"That Lourdes, I think that she is here," said Du Pré. He got up and he went outside.

A big black eighteen-wheeler, bright with chrome, flames painted on the hood, tinted windows. It ground slowly up the dirt street and it came up to Du Pré and stopped.

The passenger door opened and Lourdes stepped down on the fender and then to the running board. She pulled a duffel bag after her. She dropped the duffel bag on the ground and then she jumped down.

Lourdes looked at Du Pré.

"Momma here, yes?" she said, warily.

"Bart take her to talk to that dumb boyfriend of yours," said Du Pré. "Me, I don't like to be Sean this moment."

"He is a dumb shit," said Lourdes.

"Yeah, well," said Du Pré. "He is not a very happy dumb shit this time, you bet."

Lourdes shrugged.

A young man dressed all in black, cowboy hat, boots, belt with a big turquoise-and-silver buckle, rings, watch, bracelet, came round from the far side of the big truck. He was blond and moustached and bearded. He stood by the front of his truck, loose and relaxed.

"This your friend, here?" said Du Pré.

"She don't like me so good," said the trucker. "I give her a choice, she could either tell me how to get where she lived, or I could hand her off to the juvie cops. She bitched about it some, but here we are."

Du Pré looked at the guy. The man was smiling a little and his bright blue eyes were twinkling.

All right, thought Du Pré, we got very lucky this time.

He walked over to the trucker and he stuck out his hand. The trucker shook it.

"Du Pré."

"Challis."

"Found her at a truck stop in Spokane," said Challis. "I was . . . well, I just thought I'd bring her here. Didn't know if I bought her a bus ticket she'd use it. And them juvie cops can be kinda nasty."

Du Pré nodded.

"You headed, Chicago?" said Du Pré.

Challis shook his head.

"Seattle," he said.

Well, thought Du Pré, here is some gent, he turn around and drive seven, eight hundred miles take a dumb kid home. Turn around, drive back.

Du Pré glanced over. Lourdes and the priest had gone into the house.

"I thank you," said Du Pré.

"Happy to," said Challis. He pulled a pack of smokes from his shirt pocket and he lit one.

"Uh," said Du Pré. "You spend a lot, diesel, can I give you some money?"

"Nope," said Challis. "All taken care of."

"Her mother will want to thank you," said Du Pré. "She be back in a minute."

"Well," said Challis. "Her mother comes back she'll be takin' a chunk outta the kid's ass, don't need me. I'll be on my way presently."

The man's soft drawl was Montana's own.

"Coffee?" said Du Pré.

"Nope," said Challis. "I just stretch a little here. Got to highball make the freight run there pretty close to time. I called, told 'em I had a little trouble, I'd be along presently. The thing ain't full of hearts ready to transplant, so I suppose folks will get on a couple days later."

They smoked.

"Pret' good of you," said Du Pré.

38

"Oh," said Challis. "Not really. I had a kid sister, she took off a few years ago. Shelly. That was her name."

Du Pré waited, knowing.

"Finally found her last year. What was left of her, anyway. She was a nice kid. Little wild. Loved children. Would've made a good mother."

Du Pré nodded.

"We got this bastard now," Challis went on. "I wonder maybe he was the one killed Shelly."

Du Pré nodded.

"You're Gabriel Du Pré," said Challis. "I hear you maybe are looking for the same man I'd like to meet."

Du Pré looked at Challis. The blue eyes were gray now and cold as the moon.

"Here's my card," said Challis, handing one to Du Pré. "Number on it's the cellular phone. Got a tape machine, everything. You just call me any old time. I run the Hi-Line pretty much. Sometimes Chicago to Seattle on the interstate. Haulin' goods. Lookin' for something."

Du Pré nodded.

Challis dropped his cigarette in the dirt. He ground it out with his boot and he got up in his cab and the big diesel thrummmbbbed and the huge truck moved away.

You damn bet I call you, Du Pré thought.

Bart's Rover was coming up the street.

❧ CHAPTER 9 ❧

That's very good news," said Harvey Wallace. "I didn't care to have any more phone time with your Madelaine. Lovely woman. I don't like having her mad at me."

"Yeah," said Du Pré. "It is always better, life, when Madelaine is not mad at you."

Du Pré was sitting out on the porch of Bart's house using a portable telephone. He didn't know how it worked. He didn't want to.

"Reason I called, though, is Agent Pidgeon is going to be out your way, her with the gorgeous knockers, asking questions about this swell guy you have dropping the bodies in the sagebrush. Agent Pidgeon is personally very pissed off at that guy. She tells me no man can quite understand how pissed off she is on account of we are not the prey of these predators. She has a point."

Du Pré rolled a smoke with his left hand. He licked the paper.

"So I told her to call you *after* she calls Benny," said Harvey.

"OK," said Du Pré. "I don't got much to tell her, though."

"Benetsee ever show up?" said Harvey.

"No," said Du Pré. "I thought I saw him, at a powwow, over by some trees, but when I get there he is gone."

"They are like that," said Harvey. He meant medicine people.

"Yeah," said Du Pré. "Me, I give a lot to talk to Benetsee about his dreams about now."

"Well . . ." said Harvey.

"One more thing," said Du Pré. "I just think of it. This trucker, he is a nice guy, bring Lourdes back OK. I like him. He say that he had a little sister, they found her dead after she had been missing a long time. He tell me, call him, I need anything. He drives the Hi-Line and some Chicago, Seattle stuff."

"Oh, great," said Harvey. "We got an avenging angel in a big rig."

"He tell me his name, Challis."

"What does he look like?" said Harvey, sharply.

"Blond, six feet, blue eyes, middle thirties maybe," said Du Pré. "Got tattoos on his hands and forearms, I don't remember what they were."

"Oh, yeah," said Harvey. "I know Rolly Challis."

"Shelly and Rolly?" said Du Pré.

"Makes you wonder why more kids don't off their parents," said

40

Harvey. "But Rolly is no laughing matter. I almost busted him, but he done got clean away. I would dearly love to bust him. Can't, though."

"OK," said Du Pré. "Why you want to bust him."

"There was a time . . . look, the guy robbed banks. Damn good at it, too. Never hurt a soul. Most of those assholes are so stupid they can't piss and whistle at the same time. Not Rolly. Never worked with anyone else, so we couldn't get an accomplice to rat him out. Didn't leave us anything nice, like fingerprints or blood or hair. Tell you about one of them. Little dink town called Bigfork, it's gone to yuppies now, up on Flathead Lake? They had a little bank there. There was never any money to speak of in that damned bank but one time a year. They grow a lot of cherries up there, and the bank had to have cash to take care of the checks that the growers wrote the pickers. Cherry season lasts a week, maybe ten days. They had about a quarter mil in small unmarked there, that one fucking Friday, and some guy in a ski mask comes in and takes it. Soft voice, Montana drawl, big gun—I'd bet Rolly didn't even load the damn thing—in and out in five minutes with a couple garbage bags full of twenties. He run everybody into one corner and loaded up, leaving the dye packet bombs. Pretty smooth. Out the door, into a car he'd stolen just ten minutes before, they find the car an hour later on a Forest Service road and the bandit is solid gone."

"Oh," said Du Pré.

"Now," said Harvey, "I don't want you to get the impression that I hate Rolly or anything. He's a pretty nice guy, never did any of the things the assholes do. Just robbed banks some until he got a stake together and then he quit. I think. I got no proof. Or his ass would be in Walla Walla, but there it is. Actually, it could be a lot worse. Guy has brains and balls."

Du Pré laughed. Then so did Harvey.

"I like him," said Harvey. "Dropped by, asked him a few questions once, he looked me in the eye and lied and we both knew it. Now, there wasn't a thing I could do, unless he decided to get clean with Jesus and confess, but Rolly ain't the religious type and he just wouldn't help me throw his ass in the pen for twenty years."

"Yeah," said Du Pré. "Well, neither would I."

"So he made us look like assholes," said Harvey. "Big fucking deal."

They chatted a few more minutes and Du Pré hung up.

Agent Pidgeon, Du Pré thought. My Madelaine, she will like this.

Du Pré looked off toward the lower pasture. Forty head of horses were running flat out across the rolling yellow grass. There was a lot of green in it, there was still water and it was still raining some.

Good horses. Booger Tom had bought them over time. He pretty much ran the place, to lose money, so Bart could take some tax write-offs. Booger Tom said there was just nothin' in the world easier than losing money in the cattle business.

And Bart about had a cow himself when Booger Tom made money. Quite a lot of money, in the cattle business. The perverse old bastard.

"I never been able to do nothing right," said Tom, straight-faced, when Bart complained. "There it is. So shoot me."

Then Booger Tom had said he didn't like cows all that much and he was sure he could lose money in the horse business.

"You made seven hundred fucking thousand dollars!" Bart had yelled, "Which cost me three million!"

"You want to lose money or not?" said Booger Tom, and he grinned.

Du Pré chuckled. He looked again and saw Booger Tom on a big roan gelding chasing the horses. Man was probably seventy-five and he rode like a rider. No effort.

Du Pré went in the house and he got a drink of water and some ham from the fridge and an apple and he ate out on the porch. He picked his teeth with a sliver. He looked down at the deck he had built and noticed a few of the pegs had started and were fair. Water in the punch holes. He'd have to pound them down. Reglue them. Maybe just cut them off, they had lasted a couple years and a few were always not quite right.

Du Pré went to the tool barn and he got a hammer and he came back and whacked the pegs down flush with the redwood.

It was a beautiful cool, sunny day.

A golden eagle hung high in the sky, drifting.

Now, Du Pré thought, where that god damned Benetsee is? I need to talk to him.

Du Pré heard a siren, far off. It faded. Came back. Faded.

The hills were muffling it.

Headed this way.

Why? Someone is sick.

Du Pré looked down toward Cooper.

He saw flashing blue lights crest a hill and dip out of sight.

Shit.

Benny's car.

Du Pré went into the house and he got a canvas jacket and he filled a water bottle and put some jerked meat in his pocket. He went out to his car and he started it and turned around and headed down the long county road toward Benny.

Du Pré stopped in a snowplow turnout and he waited.

Two minutes later Benny's car came flying over the crest of the near hill. Du Pré leaned against his old cruiser. He smoked.

Benny saw him and he slowed and turned in.

Du Pré walked to Benny's car. He saw Benny's white face through the window. Benny fumbled with the electric window openers for a moment, too upset to do small things properly.

"Du Pré . . ." said Benny.

"We got another one?" said Du Pré.

"Yeah," said Benny.

"Well," said Du Pré. "Why don't you call me?"

"I needed some time to think," said Benny. Or not think, just drive.

"Where?" said Du Pré.

"Dry wash near town," said Benny. "Cooper, I mean."

"OK," said Du Pré.

"Been there a while," said Benny. "That little Morse girl who disappeared five, six years ago?"

Du Pré nodded. He remembered that one well. The child was five or six, had gone out to play a little more at dusk. No one ever saw her again. She might have been taken by a mountain lion, there were some fresh tracks in the area. That was all that anyone could come up with. The cat ate all of her.

Mountain lions did that. Ate children, skulls, everything.

The child was the daughter of a schoolteacher. The schoolteacher had stayed another year and then had moved away. Du Pré didn't know where she went.

"OK," said Du Pré. "We go there."

Benny turned around and Du Pré got in his car and he pulled up behind Benny.

Benny roared off, a crazy speed for the bad road.

The two of them shot down toward Cooper.

Benny slowed near town and he pulled off the road into a big pasture which had a rutted track going cross it to a slash in the earth a half mile away.

Another Sheriff's car was there, lights slowly flashing.

Benny and Du Pré drove slowly over the rocks and ruts up to the other car. They parked and got out.

Du Pré walked up to the edge of the dry wash.

Benny's deputy was down in the bottom, near a rusted fifty-five-gallon drum.

He was on his hands and knees, vomiting.

✤ CHAPTER 10 ✤

I hate these motherfuckers," said Agent Pidgeon.

She was looking at the photographs of little Karen Morse. What the killer had left of little Karen. Among other things, he had skinned the child and carefully rolled the skin up in salt and tied the package with the ribbons the little girl had had in her hair.

Du Pré looked at the FBI agent. She was six feet tall, slender, with big tits and a narrow waist and legs, legs, legs. Heart-shaped face and big brown eyes. Long pale brown hair. Caramel. She had some Indian blood in her, long earlobes. Thick gold earrings. A nice stainless steel Sig Sauer combat 9mm. in a holster hung low under her arm. She had her fitted jacket off. She was smoking.

"Skeleton was in the bottom of the barrel, this was wrapped up and just lying off in the brush, right?" said Agent Pidgeon. "We'll go out there tomorrow."

You and me and Madelaine go out there tomorrow, thought Du Pré, is how that will work, until Madelaine and you have a little talk. Not that you would want anything to do with a Métis grandfather, but what I think don't mean shit here, yes.

"Uh," said Benny. "Ma'am, do you want to get some dinner?"

"S'pose so," said Agent Pidgeon. "Keep up my strength. Thanks. I get a little jacked, I see things like this."

"Yeah," said Benny. "I know what you mean."

"Fuck," said Agent Pidgeon.

Benny's glance kept returning to Agent Pidgeon's tits. He was helpless before their magnificence.

"Yeah, right, food," said Agent Pidgeon. She slipped her jacket on and she picked up her attaché case.

The rest of her luggage was piled out in the front of the Sheriff's office. Three suitcases and a couple big aluminum trunks.

"You screen the crime scene?" she said. "Run everything through a sieve?"

"No," said Benny.

Agent Pidgeon nodded.

"Well," she said. "Maybe there's nothing there. You . . . I dunno. Look, I don't mean to stalk in here, be a hotshot asshole from the FBI. But maybe he dropped something. Maybe there's a piece of jewelry. Some damn thing. You got Boy Scouts? Let them help out?"

"Help out how?" said Benny.

"We could dig up all the earth around the site," said Agent Pidgeon, "and run it through a screen."

45

"Oh," said Benny. "I guess so."

Agent Pidgeon looked at Benny. She looked at Du Pré. She shrugged.

"Yeah," she said. "I am a little hungry."

When they went out the door of the Sheriff's office they saw the tan government sedan that Pidgeon had been driving being towed to the garage. Pidgeon had driven at such a rate of speed from Billings that the car had blown up twenty miles down the highway. One rod and piston had gone right through the side of the engine.

Du Pré had been closer, so he fetched her after she called Benny's office on the phone.

When he had pulled up to the steaming car, off in the barrow pit, he noticed all the luggage piled neatly by the roadside. Agent Pidgeon was sitting on one of the suitcases, legs nicely crossed, smoking a cigarette and looking like an ad for some filter-tip brand.

"You Indian?" she said, when Du Pré had loaded her luggage, with her help, and loaded her, and driven off.

"Métis," said Du Pré, "French, Scottish, Cree, Chippewa—we are the Mixed Bloods."

"Hum," said Agent Pidgeon, "I'm a Redbone myself. Black, Cherokee, white, Mexican, French. . . ."

"Oh," said Du Pré. "You are Louisiana."

"Some of my folks were," said Pidgeon. "Me, I'm pure California surfin' girl. Grew up in Coronado. Drink Dos Equis, get tan. Wear gold chains."

"How you get to the FBI?" said Du Pré.

"They needed me," said Agent Pidgeon. "I'm so many nice minority groups. Besides, after Georgetown Law School I was pretty well convinced that I would be a lot happier putting scum in jail than I would be keeping them out of it. Did a stint in the D.C. Public Defender's Office. That'll do it for ya."

"Oh," said Du Pré.

"I am not a nice person," said Agent Pidgeon.

"Uh," said Du Pré.

"You seem like a smart man," said Agent Pidgeon.

"Huh?" said Du Pré.

"Yup," said Agent Pidgeon.

Du Pré shrugged. He rolled himself a cigarette with his left hand as he was shooting down the highway at eighty.

Agent Pidgeon looked at him doing it.

Du Pré lit his cigarette.

"Let me try that," said Agent Pidgeon.

Du Pré handed her the papers and the little bag of Bull Durham.

"You are a psychologist?" said Du Pré.

"What do you think?" said Agent Pidgeon.

"That Georgetown is a pretty good law school, yes?" said Du Pré.

"They think so," said Agent Pidgeon.

"Where you get your psychology degree?"

"Columbia," said Agent Pidgeon. "They thought they were a pretty good psychology school, they said so."

Du Pré laughed.

"OK," said Agent Pidgeon. "What matters to me is we catch this guy and send him up forever or fry the fucker, either one'll do. If we do that, then they were good schools, if not, they ain't shit."

Du Pré roared.

"Harvey said I'd like you," said Agent Pidgeon. "He also said you were a good guy and not to beat up on Benny Klein, who is a good guy, too, but not that much of a cop."

"Benny, he is a small rancher," said Du Pré. "He is maybe too kind a man to do this well."

"I imagine he does fine," Agent Pidgeon had said.

Du Pré thought about all this while he drove Agent Pidgeon to the bar in Toussaint, which had the only real food in the area.

There were a few people in the bar. Agent Pidgeon looked around the shabby big room, at the mangy deer and elk heads and the ratty bear skin nailed to one wall. She nodded.

She walked over to the bar and leaned over to Susan Klein and she said a few words and then she fished a little gift out of her attaché case. Susan laughed and took it and she turned it around in her hand and then she took the ribbon and paper off it. She lifted the lid of the little box and took out a pair of silver earrings, big circles of metal with strands of beads hanging in the center hole.

Du Pré looked on and he grinned. That Harvey Weasel Fat, always sucking up to them women. Smart man, that Harvey.

The door opened behind Du Pré and Madelaine came in with Lourdes in tow. They were laughing. They hugged Du Pré.

"That is that Agent Pidgeon," said Madelaine, hissing into Du Pré's ear. "Some set of tits she got, there. I think maybe I watch the two of you pret' good."

"She don't want some broke-down Métis," said Du Pré.

"Good thing, too," said Madelaine.

Agent Pidgeon had turned around and she was looking at Du Pré and Madelaine and Lourdes. She came over.

"Madelaine?" said Agent Pidgeon. "Harvey said that you were the best thing about Du Pré, here. And this is Lourdes?"

"Yes. Yes."

"Um," said Agent Pidgeon. "We could get a table."

They found an empty table with four chairs and they sat. Susan Klein came over.

"I know what they want, dear," she said. "How about you?"

"Red wine?" said Pidgeon.

"Cabernet?" said Susan. "It's pretty good. What I drink."

"Wonderful."

"Steaks are good," said Susan. "The special is gone, sorry."

"Rare," said Pidgeon.

"OK," said Susan. She went off.

"Harvey sends his love," said Pidgeon.

"Ah, he is such a good dancer," said Madelaine.

Du Pré looked at the ceiling.

"Nice man, too," said Madelaine.

"Harvey?" said Pidgeon. "Harvey maybe changes he comes out here. Back there he's a giant pain in the ass. Always staring at my tits and wondering when I am going to get what he needs out of the computer."

"He is a guy," said Madelaine. "They got only the two heads, think with the little one, they all belong, hospitals."

"Mama!" said Lourdes.

"My daughter, she wants me in a cage," said Madelaine.

Lourdes was blushing.

Why she run away? thought Du Pré. He hadn't been told.

"Lourdes," said Pidgeon. "This Challis guy who brought you back here? How did he pick you up?"

Lourdes looked down at her lap. Her lower lip quivered.

Pidgeon reached over and she patted Lourdes's hand.

"It's OK, honey," she said, "as long as you're all right."

Du Pré looked at Lourdes.

I wonder any of us know any of us, he thought.

✣ CHAPTER 11 ✣

Du Pré threw a shovelful of earth scraped from the hard ground near the barrel against the sieve. Booger Tom played a hose that ran from a spray tank on a big flatbed truck against the earth. The soil ran yellow from the screen. Gravels gleamed.

Nothing.

They had been doing this for three days.

They had found one post from an earring for a pierced ear.

Little Karen Morse had not had pierced ears.

Du Pré thought about the skinned child. She had been white-blond.

Five years old.

He threw another shovelful of earth against the sloping screen.

Bart and a couple of the ranch hands were walking slowly on each

49

side of the rutted track that led back to the dry wash, stooping to look at anything out of the ordinary. There were a few condoms left by kids who had pulled off here to fuck. Beer cans and bottles, a couple bright paper bags that once held potato chips.

Booger Tom had spotted a hank of the child's hair stuck on a sagebrush a hundred feet away.

"Moved wrong," said Booger Tom. Tracking, you looked for what should not be there and was, or what should be there and was not.

Tracking.

Du Pré shoved the tip of the shovel's blade toward a thick old sagebrush trunk. The earth parted easily. Something gleamed.

A chain, the sort that made a bracelet. The links were bent flat.

Du Pré whistled.

He dropped down on his hands and knees and he stared hard at the chain peeking out from the broken earth.

A green gemstone sparkled.

"What you got, there?" said Booger Tom. He had come after he shut off the hose.

"A chain," said Du Pré. He took a pencil from his pocket and he put it through the loop of chain and he tugged it away from the earth that held it.

Several clods came up with it. Du Pré saw a knife blade, a stainless-steel one, short and wide.

"I'll get some bags," said Booger Tom. He limped off toward the cab of the truck.

Du Pré waited and he stared.

When Tom came back Du Pré dropped the bracelet into the first of the locking plastic bags. He took a pair of folding pliers from his pocket and he jabbed the needlenose points around the knife blade and pulled the knife away from the soil.

Buried about three inches deep, Du Pré thought. Scratch this earth and it breaks up like dry bread.

Du Pré looked at the knife. Stainless-steel, three-inch blade, double-sided. Black plastic handle. He looked at the brand name but it had been ground off.

Du Pré grunted. He dropped the knife in a plastic bag and sealed it.

He tugged a ring out of the dirt.

The metal was discolored, the gem a piece of dime-store glass.

The sort of trinket a poor girl would buy for herself.

Du Pré stood up. He picked up the shovel and pushed it into the ground. The soil broke easily.

He carried the shovelful to the sieve. He tossed it on the screen. Booger Tom hosed it down.

Five earrings.

Thin cheap silver chain gone to greenish black.

A penny.

Du Pré put them all in the same bag.

Du Pré and Tom worked the spot carefully, shoveling around the trunk of the sagebrush.

They found one small brass key, of the size for a jewelry box.

Nothing else.

Agent Pidgeon arrived in the tan government car. Wally the mechanic had stuck a new used engine in it. It took him about half a day.

"Paydirt," said Pidgeon, holding up the bags. "There won't be anything else. This guy is very careful."

Bart and the ranch hands were standing near. They'd walked the whole half mile of road without seeing a thing that could be useful.

"It's him," said Pidgeon. "He dumps the bodies and he buries a knife and some effects nearby. The effects usually don't square with the bodies. I expect he buries the trophies from the last killing with the next, and so forth. Only keeps the most current mementos."

"Trophies?" said Du Pré.

Pidgeon nodded. "Souvenirs," she said, "of his triumphs. Young women are the enemy. When he kills one, he wins. My profile is fairly standard. This guy is white, unmarried, thirty-five to forty. He's compulsive about cleanliness. He's quiet. He's not very skilled socially, and feels very clumsy around women. He probably doesn't drink or smoke and certainly never takes street drugs. He is, on the surface, very religious, though all his talk of it is about sin and atonement—he's providing atonement for these poor women. He's physically very strong, because he fears weakness of any kind. He's probably been in some trouble with the law as a juvenile."

"What kind of trouble?" said Du Pré.

"Arson, petty theft, violence to kids younger than he is. He would have tortured animals and killed them though he may never have been caught at it. May never have been caught with the other. Probably came from a poor and violent home. Single parent, most likely his mother. She can't, for whatever reason, offer love. I bet this guy has a young sister who he thinks got all the love."

Pidgeon lit a cigarette.

"He kills with a knife thrust to the juncture of the spine and the skull. That's why he uses these short blades. The victim is bound. He may have intercourse with the body. Probably can't, can't get it up at any time. If he goes with a prostitute, she'll maybe suck him off, but he'll do so rarely. If she can't manage to get him off, he'll kill her even if he has to wait."

"Sweet guy," said Booger Tom.

"Fellow Americans," said Agent Pidgeon. "About forty of 'em plying their trade at any given time. We maybe catch half of them."

"Like that Ted Bundy?" said Du Pré.

"Dunno," said Pidgeon. "But I suspect this guy is a lot smarter than Bundy. I suspect this guy is very smart indeed, and he has the instincts of a wild creature."

"Why smart?" said Du Pré.

"Um," said Pidgeon. "He does some of the things that various of these types do, but never so much they provide us with a weakness. Like the trophies. He keeps a few. There is probably a number he allows himself. He never keeps the knife he kills with. The knives have always been so thoroughly cleaned there aren't any residues on them. He always uses this kind of knife. The handle is tight and impermeable plastic. Blood can't seep in between the blade and the handle. He hides the bodies where they will be undiscovered for a long time. He isn't taunting us directly. He's not playing chicken with us. He doesn't want to get caught."

"You're damn right there," said Booger Tom.

"No," said Pidgeon. "They mostly do. See, most of them get crazier and crazier and more and more careless. They've been able to milk the system for bennies, con the shrinks. They want to get caught and be famous. They think they're unique. Living National Treasures, you bet."

"Social workers done this," said Tom.

"Yeah, right," said Pidgeon.

"Well," said Tom. "Ever' time ya turn around someone is getting off scot-free because his mother pulled the tit too quick or something."

"Whatever," said Pidgeon. "This guy worries me, though. They all worry me, but this guy really worries me."

"OK," said Du Pré. "But why?"

"He's very smart," said Pidgeon. "He's probably an autodidact. He reads a lot. High IQ. If he works, it's at a highly skilled job where he doesn't have much to do with people. He doesn't have close friends, but people will think of him as a friend. He'll be thoughtful and ingratiating. He'll wear clothes in muted tones. He doesn't talk a lot and when he does it will be about inoffensive subjects. He won't argue with anyone. He won't get into rows in bars. He doesn't vote. He has a driver's license and a Social Security card, but no charge cards. He always pays cash and in small bills. He doesn't save receipts. He most likely cuts the labels out of his clothes. He wears jogging shoes, or the heavier walking shoes, in dark brown or green. Black is too much of a statement. He wears glasses, probably black frames, heavy ones, with ordinary lenses. No bombardier glasses for this boy. May not even need them. He's clean-shaven. He gets his hair cut short regularly. He may still live with his mother, or, if she's dead, with a sister or other female relation. He always makes his bed. Unlike most of you guys, when he does his laundry he bleaches his whites and keeps them separate. He cleans up after himself. He knows a lot about women and he hates them if they are young and pretty and innocent or if he thinks they are whores."

"How you know all this?" said Tom.

"I read fucking tea leaves," said Pidgeon.

"I thought so," said Booger Tom.

"Let's go get a drink," said Pidgeon. "I'm buying. Thank you for all this stuff."

"I'll take the rig back and meet you to town," said Booger Tom.

"Du Pré?" said Pidgeon.

"My car is in Toussaint," said Du Pré. "I come out with Tom, he had to come to town to get a belt for the truck."

"Ride with me," said Pidgeon. "I need to talk to you anyway."

"Social workers and fairy shrinks," said Booger Tom.

"Fuck off, you old bastard," said Agent Pidgeon.

⚜ CHAPTER 12 ⚜

"She is some pistol," said Du Pré, into the telephone.

"Oh, yes," said Harvey Wallace. "I would dearly love to make a dozen little Redbone Blackfeet with her, but Angela would object and she's Sioux and you know what they do to unfaithful husbands."

"You are married?" said Du Pré.

"Twenty-seven years," said Harvey. "Six kids. Lovely wife. Two dogs. Home in the burbs. A station wagon and a Jeep Cherokee."

"Oh," said Du Pré.

"Yeah," said Harvey. "I'm hopelessly middle-class. And I don't like buffalo meat. Or horse meat. Or chokecherry jam. Makes my teeth hurt. Moccasins make my feet hurt. Poor-ass Indian."

"Uh," said Du Pré. "Well, she did tell me a lot about this guy, she thinks she knows this stuff about him."

"If she says the guy does this or that, he does this or that," said Harvey. "She's a damn fine psychologist and then on top of that she's intuitive as hell."

"What's intuitive?" said Du Pré.

"Senses things without thinking them through."

"Yeah," said Du Pré, "she is a woman, you bet."

"Whatever," said Harvey. "Under law, there is no difference between the brains of men and the brains of women."

"Laws are pretty much bullshit," said Du Pré.

"I wish you would quit talking like that," said Harvey. "I have a sick feeling that if you find the guy he's gonna have more holes in him than a fucking colander and then we'll have to arrest you and try you and toss you in Walla Walla. For a long time."

Du Pré said nothing.

"Benetsee back?" said Harvey.

"No," said Du Pré. "I do not know where he is." The old bastard, may he drop slowly through all the levels of hell, frying while he falls.

"Shit," said Harvey. "Agent Pidgeon needs to meet him."

"Me, I need to talk to him," said Du Pré. "But I can't find out where he has gone."

"He's his own guy, for sure," said Harvey. "Well, Agent Pidgeon did call from Billings and she raised merry hell down there with the cops who screwed up some evidence."

"I like her," said Du Pré.

"She's a good one," said Harvey. "By the way, you talk to Challis at all? He's on my mind some."

"No," said Du Pré, "I have not."

"Well," said Harvey. "No more bodies turn up there, I hope, you can maybe work on what you got. I wish to Christ we knew more about time."

"Yeah," said Du Pré, not quite knowing what Harvey meant.

"When this guy is dumping them. Time we find them, they've been out there for months, usually. Your three were under the snow until late, it was a late spring."

"Four," said Du Pré.

"I haven't forgotten," said Harvey. "Poor little Karen was skinned and her skeleton was fleshed out. All sorts of knife marks on the bones."

"Jesus," said Du Pré.

"I want this guy alive, Du Pré," said Harvey. "I have heard bad rumors about you. Some guy up in New York State."

"Ah," said Du Pré.

"Ah?" said Harvey. "OK, I'll go now. Don't make me sad, my man, I beg of you."

"OK," said Du Pré.

"Enough of this bullshit," said Harvey. "I'm calling Madelaine."

Du Pré hung up.

He went outside on the porch again.

Harvey and Pidgeon are not telling me everything, Du Pré thought, they play to win. I kill this asshole, they will try to get me.

Him call Madelaine, she tell him her Du Pré do what he is gonna do, which, for Madelaine, would be kill this bastard anyway.

Then everybody's babies safe from him.

Lots of others out there, though.

Forty of them, any given time.

Pret' bad people.

I wish Benetsee would show up.

Du Pré rolled a cigarette. He whistled a little in between drags. This afternoon he would go to the bar in Toussaint and fiddle with a couple of cousins down from Canada.

Big family, mine, Du Pré thought. Indian family. These cousins they are from people come down here with my great-great-grandfather, then they go to North Dakota and back up to Canada. Always in the Red River country. I like that country, sings in my bones.

Goes to Hudson's Bay.

Wonder how them whales are doing.

Wonder that Hydro-Quebec kill that River of the Whale yet. Damn it. I should ask Bart, he sends money to fight that.

The fields of winter wheat were ripening now. July. They were going to red-gold and that hard red wheat was getting ready for the harvest. Ring good on the shovel, that hard red wheat.

Du Pré remembered threshing, the combine crews, everybody itching from the chaff. The streams of dark red winter wheat shooting out of the pipes and into the trucks lumbering along on the side of the combines. Sell all the hard red wheat you could grow, anybody. Make pasta, them good noodles. One-fifth protein. Come from Russia, that hard red wheat.

The Dukhobors brought it, I hear.

Du Pré liked the Dukhobors, a pacifist Russian sect. If a Dukhobor got really mad with you, they undressed. I will not fight you, I am naked before your violence, but I am mad at you.

The Mennonites, during the First World War they came and got the men and hung them from handcuffs on a pipe till their shoulders dislocated, because they wouldn't fight.

The Hutterites. Good farmers, shrewd traders.

Good people, just don't have much truck with the rest of the world. Who can blame them?

Du Pré flicked his smoke out into the yard. The grass was meadow grass, already drying and yellowing and going dormant.

Du Pré got his fiddle and he went to his old cruiser and he got in and turned around and went down the long drive.

That Bart he is off digging a big irrigation ditch with Popsicle, his lime green diesel shovel. One we find the answer to his brother's death with. Find a lot of things. Find out more truth than maybe we want to know. That is the thing about truth, there is only too much or not enough.

Du Pré drove slowly, windows down, listening to the meadowlarks trill. Big yellow-breasted birds got a black wishbone on their chests. He glanced over and saw a brilliant bluebird, winged sapphire, sitting on the fence post its house was nailed to.

Got to get the hole the right size in the house or you got starlings. Yuppie birds, maybe. Lots of squawk and sharp elbows. No taste.

Du Pré was in no hurry. It took him an hour to go the twenty miles to town. He went to Madelaine's.

He parked and went in the front door.

"Du Pré!" Madelaine called. "There is a box for you there!"

Du Pré looked at the box on the coffee table. Shirt box.

Madelaine, she make me another shirt.

"OK," said Du Pré. "I see, shirt box."

"Smarty," said Madelaine from the bathroom. "You look in that, see how your woman love you."

Du Pré lifted off the top.

Bright red shirt with black piping and fiddles over the pockets made of porcupine quills. The shirt was heavy silk. Du Pré picked it up. A red silk Métis sash was folded underneath. Fiddles on that, too, and DU PRÉ on the back in black beads. Very fine beads. Two circlets on each side with coyotes howling at yellow moons on them. Du Pré felt something crinkle in the sash's pocket, on an end that hung down. He fished out a dollar bill.

Bad luck to give an empty purse.

Madelaine came out of the bathroom. She was wearing a heavy turquoise silk/satin shirt with yellow flowers embroidered on it in fine beads, a long yellow skirt, and yellow cowboy boots. Her rings were all turquoise and silver and coral.

Her hair was in two long braids. Beaver fur wrapped around them.

"You play that good music, eh?" said Madelaine.

Du Pré nodded. He was shrugging into the shirt. He put his fiddle rosin in the pocket of the sash and he stuck the other end through the loops on his jeans.

He drove down to the bar. Two old cars with North Dakota plates stood outside. Cousins.

Du Pré was a little late and his cousins were picking and singing already. He tuned his fiddle and then joined them.

They played the old voyageur stuff, the longing songs of men far from their women, thinking that maybe they would not see them again.

Long time ago, on the lakes bordered by the deep black woods.
The Company of Gentlemen Adventurers of Hudson's Bay.
The Métis voyageurs.
Red River.

✤ CHAPTER 13 ✤

Round midnight Du Pré and his cousins were playing very tight and the crowd had thinned to those who simply loved the music. The whoopers had gotten drunk and left. Madelaine was looking at Du Pré with her bright and saucy black eyes and she would smile when he looked at her.

Got plans for you, her face said.

Du Pré grinned and rosined his bow.

There is nothing left of us but songs and stories finally, Du Pré thought.

Even maybe when the earth is ice again and the Red River sleeps for a long time. Missouri, she used to flow to Hudson's Bay, but ice come and now she goes to the Gulf of Mexico.

I am a man, but we are not very big.

" 'Baptiste's Lament'!" said Sonny, the accordion player.

Du Pré nodded. The song was about a young voyageur who misses his love and he sees her in the moon on the water, smiling. And when he gets home she is dead, and he drowns when he sees her in the moon on the water again, swimming down after her, singing.

Sad song.

They took a break. Du Pré was leaning up against the bar kissing Madelaine when Susan Klein tapped him on the shoulder and handed him the telephone. Du Pré looked at Susan. She shrugged.

"Eh," said Du Pré.

"Du Pré," said a soft drawling voice.

"Who is this?" said Du Pré.

"Rolly Challis," said the soft voice. "I'm in Browning. I'll be at Raster Creek in four hours. Could you meet me there?"

Five in the fucking morning.

"Sure," said Du Pré. "You got something."

"Maybe," said Rolly. "Some things I need to talk over with you anyway. Sorry about the time but that's my run. I can take a couple hours there, highball later."

"Yah," said Du Pré, "I be there."

The phone clicked.

"Girlfriend?" said Madelaine.

"Yah," said Du Pré, "She meet me at five in the morning. I got time for you before, maybe after. I am busy man, you know."

Madelaine smiled suddenly. She reached up and took Du Pré's right earlobe in her teeth and she bit it softly.

"You see that man brought my Lourdes back?" she hissed. Du Pré's ear was a little wet. "You thank him for me. No, I will not go, but sometime I like to thank him, smile at him with my face."

Du Pré nodded.

Sonny and Bassman were chatting with a couple pretty women from Cooper. Everybody looked happy. Be even happier later.

"That Sonny, he better not get tangled up with that La Fant woman," said Madelaine. "She is some twister. She take guys, make them crazy. She likes to watch them fight about her."

Du Pré shrugged. My cousin, he is forty, I never hardly know him he is not fighting over some crazy woman. He like it, help get his dick up, I guess.

"That Bassman," Madelaine went on. "He is talking sweet to Alyse. She is nice, have a bad time, men. She picks bad men."

Bassman, he collect women all over the place. Someday they all have nice lunch, together, there, get up a posse, go cut off Bassman's balls and then hang him from a tree, sit down, drink beer while he bleeds to death dangling.

My cousins want to play that way, I am not their mother, thought Du Pré, I am just a cousin. Fools.

Sonny and Bassman got back up on the little stage, grinning like dogs in a field of fresh cow shit.

Heat.

"I go now," said Du Pré. "Do some songs then we go."

"Poor Du Pré," laughed Madelaine. "You get no sleep tonight. I do while you are gone. You get back, you get no sleep then either."

"I stand it somehow," said Du Pré. He picked his fiddle up off the top of the bar and he walked to the stage and he got up and stood and listened to the rhythms Bassman was pulling out of his fretless electric bass. Some backbeat, there.

Play across the creek, Du Pré thought, sail my hat over.

He shot little icy notes into the smoky air.

People got up and they began to dance.

Madelaine came to the stage and she danced in front of Du Pré, running her tongue tip around her lips.

I hope I don't drop the beat, fucked up by my hard-on, thought Du Pré, my woman is messing with me. Some fun.

They played and people danced and they left in couples. The bar was emptied by the last song, except for a few people.

Du Pré cased up his fiddle. He shook hands with his cousins and he nodded and smiled at their women and he took Madelaine home.

After, they lay pearled with sweat, the window open and the cool night air flowing over their hot bodies.

"I got to go," said Du Pré.

"I got plans, you, you get back," murmured Madelaine.

Du Pré got up and he pulled on his clothes and boots and he went out to his old cruiser. The glass was thick with dew. Bullbats flew overhead, catching insects in the single pole light by the street. The little brown bats would be down by the water, eating mosquitoes.

Du Pré started the cruiser and he let it warm while he took an old towel and wiped the thick stippled water from the windshield. He got in and he rolled three cigarettes and laid them on the dashboard, and then a fourth he stuck in his mouth and he lit. He pulled a bottle of Canadian whiskey from under the seat and he had a stiff drink.

Keep me awake. Run on whiskey, pussy, and music. Not a bad life that I got. I say that, my Madelaine belt me in the mouth.

Du Pré turned around and he headed for the little two-lane blacktop that snaked around the foothills of the Wolf Mountains to the west of the range. It led up to the Hi-Line and came into the main stem at Raster Creek.

I did not know what Raster meant, Du Pré thought, so I ask Booger Tom. The old man snorted and said it was a corruption of "arrastra," the Spanish millwheel of heavy stone drawn round and round by burros to crush ore for roasting.

Du Pré had seen a couple of the huge stones up in the Wolfs. The Spanish had got this far north?

Why not?

The road was wet, black and snaking north into the night. Du Pré put the car up to ninety and he shot along under the blurry moon. High cloud, lot of water in the air.

The country changed. Du Pré could smell a different soil, some sour thing in the water. Several times deer froze in the headlights. Du Pré braked hard and got down to a crawl till he was past them. They might move off the road, but they might run back if the headlights blinded them.

He got to Raster Creek at a quarter to five. He got out and he sat on the warm hood of his car, smoking and drinking whiskey.

At five minutes to five he heard a big rig to the west. The truck was moving damned fast. The headlights rose ahead of the big diesel and then they blazed into view and the drive began to ring down the gears and slow the huge, heavy machine.

Big black eighteen-wheeler.

Rolly Challis brought the truck into the parking lot of the rest stop at a crawl. He stopped and the lights went out and Du Pré heard the air brakes hiss and lock and then the cab opened and Rolly dropped down, freehanded, his foot touched lightly on the rubber plate on the running board and then he was on the ground and walking quickly toward Du Pré.

Du Pré slid off the hood of his car and he walked toward Rolly.

They stopped two feet from each other.

Rolly grinned and he held out his hand.

Du Pré grinned and he shook it.

"How is Lourdes?" said Rolly.

"Oh," said Du Pré, "she is all right. She scared herself pret' good. She really ask you you want a piece of ass, Spokane?"

"Uh," said Rolly. "No, not exactly. She asked me if I would like to have her suck my *penis*. She had trouble pronouncing 'penis.' Sort of choked on it, you know. So I said, 'Little girl, you are a long damn way from home and in a lot of trouble. How bout' you tell me what's up over breakfast.' I didn't think she had a lot of time in giving blow jobs to truckers. Poor kid."

Little Lourdes, Du Pré thought. Kids, these days. I will not tell Madelaine, who would shit bobcats.

This Rolly, he is a funny man. Probably, he rob a bank, leave them all laughing.

Du Pré put the bottle of whiskey forward. Rolly shook his head.

"Thank you, though," he said.

They stood there. The sun was rising in the east, the sky was a pink curtain halfway up to heaven.

"I don't have much," said Rolly. "But I thought I'd best talk to you about it. I been driving back and forth for seven years on this route and down on the Interstate. One thing I never did, though, is look at *where* the bodies of the girls were dumped."

Rolly pulled a map from his back pocket. He stuck a small flashlight in his teeth. He went to Du Pré's cruiser and he unfolded the map. It was the western half of the United States.

There were many black X's on the map.

From Seattle to Minnesota.

From Amarillo to Calgary, Alberta.

Du Pré squinted.

The big picture.

One wide band across America, up high, the Pacific to the Great Lakes.

One wide band running north and south, along the front of the Rockies and east to the hundredth meridian.

Du Pré blinked.

"Jesus," he said. "There are maybe two of them."

"I believe so," said Rolly. He folded the map and he started to walk back to his truck.

"You go now?" said Du Pré, surprised.

"Yup," said Rolly. "When you talk to ol' Harvey Wallace, there, give him my best. Ask him about time. We need to know when the bodies were dumped."

"Yah," said Du Pré.

Rolly swung up into the cab and he moved out toward the rising sun.

✤ CHAPTER 14 ✤

I need to learn how to say 'No' better," said Bart. He looked tired. The huge lowboy trailer that had tires running nearly the entire length of it, on both sides, triple tires, sat in its spot. The giant diesel shovel, boom tucked, sat on it.

"Big job, eh?" said Du Pré.

"Biggest I have done," said Bart. "I should have another operator for Popsicle, there, but I kinda hate to hand her off to anyone."

Du Pré snorted. Bart loved his diesel shovel. Bart had, Du Pré had heard, hundreds of millions of dollars. He would have been much happier if he had been born poor. But he wasn't. It almost killed him. Du Pré remembered Bart's drunken, bloated red face the first time he had seen him. Sticking out the window of the too-big house. Booger Tom had burned the house down on Bart's orders.

Long time ago.

Bart, he had gotten drunk a few times, gotten sick, but the times got farther apart and there hadn't been one in over three years.

Du Pré nodded.

Bart, he is doing good. Wish he could find him a woman, but when he does he spends too much money on them and they feel bought and go away.

The day was already bright and hot. The eagle was high on the updraft from the fields of wheat that reached from the foothills of the Wolf Mountains behind the ranch house clear out south to where the rain fell so scantily the soil held water enough only for sagebrush.

"Wheat's up," said Booger Tom. The old man had come round the side of the house. He moved slowly now, his many injuries from a life of hard riding were coming due. Arthritis. Bones broken many times. Hands gnarled and twisted like the roots of willows.

Old cowboy, tough enough.

"I can see it's up," said Bart. "I keep telling you I want to *lose* money. I get half of the crop, if it's five-dollar wheat this year then I lose . . . oh, fuck it. Numbers, all it is."

"I keep tryin'," said Booger Tom. "Tryin' hard."

"I think," said Bart, "that the old bastard is pulling my dick."

"Give the damn wheat to charity," said Booger Tom. "Give it to them damn Rooshians."

"Yah, yah," said Bart. He went inside.

"It don't rain, then maybe harvest in a couple weeks," said Booger Tom. "Them combine crews are about a week behind."

Du Pré thought about the contract harvesters. Started down in Texas and worked north, on the road five or six months out of the year. Chaff and dust and itch and long hours. But damn good money. Good people, worked very hard.

Then, a hailstorm could come up and knock all the kernels off the heads and you got nothin'. Don't pay to comb the field.

Farming.

Ranching, you got your cows, looking for a place to hide, or your sheep, looking for a place to die.

People here, they got to be tough some.

Bart appeared at the screen door.

"Du Pré," he said, "phone. Harvey Wallace."

Du Pré flicked his butt out on the yard and he went inside and he picked up the portable phone and went back out. It crackled a little, not too bad.

"Mornin' " said Harvey.

"Yah," said Du Pré. "Nice out here. How is that Washington, D.C.?"

"Foul," said Harvey. "Sticky, full of slimy politicians and government titsuckers like me. The founding fathers hated the idea of democracy. They stuck it out in a swamp and waited for the mosquitoes to give everybody yellow fever and kill it off. I take it my man Rolly put you up to this?"

"Yah," said Du Pré.

"Well," said Harvey. "We are all low-rent riverboat gamblers here, you know, and you want to peek at our hand."

"How is that Pidgeon?" said Du Pré.

"Her of the gorgeous knockers and mean mouth?" said Harvey. "Thriving. I relayed your request to her and you know what she did?"

"Uh," said Du Pré.

"Pulled out a computer printout and said she knew you were bright and would get around to this."

"Christ," said Du Pré. "There are what, one hundred fifty of them crosses on that map? One hundred fifty?"

"A lot," said Harvey. "I doubt that all of them can be credited to one or two accounts."

"How long you know there are two of them?" said Du Pré.

"Gabriel," said Harvey, "quit spitting at me. I don't know there are two. I know there are a lot of dead bodies. I thought I would let you just run and see what you came up with. If I had told you everything we think we know, that's what you would have looked for."

"Uh," said Du Pré. "Yah, well, I do not know either. It makes me sick, all those girls, this guy, these guys, years they do this. No one sees them."

"The Green River Killer out in Washington?" said Harvey. "Killed as many as ninety. Then stopped. He died or moved away. We doubt we will ever know. I have a collage of the faces of the murdered women. It is on the wall of my office. To remind me that there is evil in the world."

"These girls," said Du Pré. "Not many of them, you know, we find out who they are."

"There are a hundred thousand runaway teenagers at least out there at any given moment," said Harvey. "Some parents are just glad that they are gone. Some parents don't have one single photograph of their child. Not one. Nothing. Some of them never report anything. They don't care. Kids are gone, not eating, taking money for booze or drugs. There are some real pieces of shit in the world. Lots of them."

"That Pidgeon," said Du Pré. "How come she has not called me?"

"She's in Europe," said Harvey, "helping out Scotland Yard. They have some bastard dismembering prostitutes around Edinburgh. Jock the Ripper, of course."

Du Pré snorted.

"We have some information," said Harvey. "But in so many cases the bodies weren't discovered until they were nothing but bones. Can't get a real good fix on that."

"How many skinned?" said Du Pré.

"Nineteen," said Harvey, "or maybe more, we just haven't found the skins."

"This guy is pretty smart," said Du Pré.

"Very smart," said Harvey. "We may never catch him."

Du Pré snorted.

"We're gonna try good, though," said Harvey. "Where is that god damned Benetsee?"

"Dunno," said Du Pré.

"He ever gone this long before?" said Harvey.

"No," said Du Pré.

"You know how to get hold of him in Canada?"

"No," said Du Pré, "I ask people, who are from there, but, one thing, I don't even know what tribe he is. I guess maybe Cree but them Cree they don't talk, each other's business at all. Very close. Anybody publish anything about their religion, they sue them. They don't want them fool New Age people bothering them."

"Like Bear Butte," said Harvey.

"Yah," said Du Pré.

Bear Butte was sacred, a vision place to many Plains tribes. So now men's movement groups and New Age idiots went there, did what they thought were Indian ceremonies. How they like it, we have a Sun Dance in the cathedral, there in Washington? We don't do that. Leave Bear Butte alone. Leave us alone.

Du Pré snorted. Here I am, bad Catholic, worse Indian. I guess I am more religious than I know.

"Shit," said Harvey. "We even tried some psychics. Not helpful. Or maybe we just can't unravel their babble. I dunno. I'd try reading animal guts like the Romans I thought'd help."

"Oh," said Du Pré, "I am forgetting, Rolly, he say to tell you hello."

Harvey laughed long.

"That son of a bitch," he said. "I can't help but like the guy. Though I'd never admit it, like every other American, when Banker Bob takes it in the shorts but good I can't help but feel a little better."

"Him got something else," said Du Pré.

"What?" said Harvey, suddenly collected.

"I don't know," said Du Pré. "I have just this hunch, you know, that he was going to tell me something else and then he changed his mind."

"Damn," said Harvey.

"One other thing," said Du Pré. "That Rolly he is a killer."

"Killed who?" said Harvey.

"Dunno he did," said Du Pré, "yet."

"You're right there," said Harvey.

"So maybe he think he get close he just do that, see if this stops," said Du Pré.

"That has worried me," said Harvey.

"Uh," said Du Pré. "He got them eyes, you know."

"Oh, yes," said Harvey.

"Maybe I am wrong," said Du Pré.

"Nope," said Harvey. "Another thing worries me."

"Uh," said Du Pré.

"You got those eyes, too, Gabriel. Remember, I'll bust your ass."

"Thanks," said Du Pré.

Harvey hung up.

✤ CHAPTER 15 ✤

Du Pré stood by the silvered pile of boards still marked with the yellow tape that the investigators had used to cordon the area off. The dirt under where the single body had been found was turned and mounded. There were bootprints on the loose soil and the marks of the feet of horses and cattle.

A coyote had scratched at the earth, perhaps scenting the meat that had rotted here. But not much. Then the coyote trotted on toward the slash of pale green where a tiny plume of water ran through the soil, coming out as a small spring miles away.

Du Pré looked up. The eagle was a speck so high in the sky that he never could have seen it had he not known exactly where to look.

That eagle, Du Pré thought, he must like it up there some. Nothing to eat, and by the time he dive the thing he is after would be ten feet under the ground.

Du Pré remembered nearly forty years before, when he was hunting with his father, Catfoot, that they had come to the edge of a meadow covered three feet deep in snow, hoping for elk on the far side. But what they saw was a deer with an eagle on its back. The big golden bird had its talons sunk in the deer's back near the neck and the eagle was flapping its wings and the deer, tongue lolling from exhaustion, was trying to run to safety but there was none.

The eagle let go and lifted and the deer stood quivering, and then the eagle's mate stooped and grasped and the deer leaped forward again.

Du Pré and his father went on. When they came back hours later, pulling the gutted carcass of a dry cow elk, the eagles were feasting on the deer.

"Them do that," said Catfoot. "Eagle, him smart bird, the gold ones. Them balds not so smart. They just steal from smaller birds."

Du Pré looked down at his feet. They seemed far away. There was a sprig of sagebrush caught in the cracked sole of his boot.

Du Pré tried to fly up with the bird, to think what this land looked like from high in the air. He could have got someone to fly him but he wasn't sure what he was looking for.

Du Pré closed his eyes.

Old house was here. Had a well, must be there, where the water ran underground.

The tracks of the tires come in here, ranchers, hunters, they go from the road off into the sagebrush past this old house that is gone, taken by the wind, to the place where there is a little saddle. Rock on either side of it is in shelves six feet high, so that is the way that you have to go to get on out into the prairie.

High plains.

Desert.

All the prophets came from the desert.

It is the place of clarity.

I have spent too much time with that Bart and his books.

This is all Red River.

The road went west, the snaking ribbon of green that followed the fractured invisible rock beneath went north. They crossed right here.

The two bodies crossed one on another were over there. Under the left arm of the cross.

Christ's right hand was on the left arm of the cross.

Du Pré shook his head.

He walked a spiraling path around the spot where the first body was found. The spiral was tight. He could see clearly ten feet or so on a side. Twenty feet wide, the ribbon of earth in his eyes unspooled.

There.

Du Pré saw some tiny leaves, little plants which had just taken root in the turned earth. Not very much turned earth. That much could be cut open here with a knife. A little trench scraped.

Filled and patted and tamped.

But the seeds knew the air and water there were enough.

They sprouted, and then . . .

There wasn't enough water.

The plant was dwarfed.

Not dead, dormant. Take a few years here, where a single season would be enough if there was enough water.

Du Pré pulled the folding tool from his belt and he opened it and selected a long file with a square tip and he locked it in place and he shut the handle.

He dug at the earth beneath the little plant.

Nothing anywhere here like that little plant.

Du Pré felt it. He wiggled the tip of the file and clods of earth broke apart.

Stainless steel gleamed.

Du Pré dug the knife out.

Short, triangular blade, black plastic handle with the brand marker scraped off.

Gleam of metal.

Gold.

Du Pré lifted out an engagement ring. Small diamond, but the gold was good, probably eighteen-carat.

71

Hopeful ring. We don't got much money starting out here, but some time, I get you a better one.

Du Pré pulled a plastic bag from his pocket and he dropped the knife and ring into it and snapped it shut, punched a little hole in the side of the bag with the file and squeezed out the air and put the bag in the pocket of his canvas jacket.

He dug around the spot, as far as the earth was disturbed.

Little piece of duct tape.

Little agate ring, silver mounting.

Two gold post earrings.

Du Pré felt the root of the sagebrush. End of the little trench.

Fucker might buy them damn knives by the gross, Du Pré thought. Hah. He buy one here, one there.

But I bet that he got a lot of them to hand. Neatly laid out in nice rows.

Duct tape.

Right hand of Christ.

I am getting something here.

Du Pré turned and he looked back through the sagebrush to the place where the woman's body had lain.

Clear view.

Knife blade pointing directly to the spot.

Du Pré got up and he walked down the line of sight, looking to the left and right.

Only place you can see this far in to where the body was.

What is it?

Old path?

No sagebrush here.

Why?

Du Pré tried to remember if the other knife blade had been pointing at the body.

Well, he thought, it would have been.

Everything this guy does he has got a reason for doing. I do not know what them reasons are but they will be there.

Tracks.

72

This guy lines things up.

He gets upset when something is out of place.

He gets really upset when he has a plan and it don't work out.

He is thinking God's plan is not doing well, women are fucking it up maybe.

This guy is trying to fix things.

Everything.

Du Pré looked back up at the eagle. Now there were two.

He walked over toward the spot where he had seen the magpie fly up so long ago. Less than a month but a long time ago.

He looked left to right. He kept looking back.

The two bodies under the right arm of Christ on the cross.

Left arm of the cross.

Everything depends on where you are standing.

He came to the spot. There wasn't so much evidence of scarring and turned earth here. They were not so thorough.

The girls had those inky jailhouse tattoos. So who cared?

Just trash in the brush.

Du Pré wondered if they had been killed at the same time.

He wondered if they were maybe sisters.

They were now.

Du Pré rolled a smoke and he lit it.

No knife here.

I know that there is no knife here.

Him, he did not do this.

These two were someone else.

They know about each other.

One of them kills north.

Other one kills east.

I am high above them looking down.

If I can bring them together, then maybe . . .

Where is Benetsee.

Where is Benetsee.

Du Pré began to whistle a tune that he realized he had never heard before. It was pretty and sad.

Try it on the fiddle.

Get it right.

The Women are Lost in the Desert.

Du Pré walked back to his old cruiser, whistling.

✤ CHAPTER 16 ✤

I don't pay that much attention to that sort of thing," said Father Van Den Heuvel. "I know that it exists and of course it probably does around here but I spend my time in pastoral duties and so forth. Why do you ask?"

Du Pré shrugged.

"I think maybe this guy have something to do with those people," said Du Pré. "The guy who is killing these girls."

"Why do you think that?" said Father Van Den Heuvel. "I perhaps could help you if I knew your thoughts."

Du Pré sucked his teeth. He rolled a cigarette.

They were sitting on the front porch of the little house Van Den Heuvel lived in. It had been willed to the church by an old woman of great faith who had pitied the priests stuck in one bare room with a tiny kitchen and bath.

"It may be that I am wrong," said Du Pré, "but that Agent Pidgeon said that this man probably felt he was doing the work of God. Killing these bad women. That he hates but he has to find a way to make his hating all right, you know. He hates because God wants him to."

"Ah," said Father Van Den Heuvel, "yes. The primitive people who join such ignorant sects are good haters, all of them. I have seen advertisements in the Billings paper for evangelists who hate practically everyone. Especially those who practice and accept abortion.

The Mother Church abhors the practice, of course, but we stop short of recommending that those who disagree with us be killed outright."

Lately you have, thought Du Pré. Lot of the history of the Church it was saying just that. Remember the Huguenots, lot of them fled here.

"OK," said Du Pré. "What would be at the right hand of Jesus, when He is on the Cross?"

"Interesting question," said Father Van Den Heuvel. "I will have to think about that."

"Um," said Du Pré. "I am going down to that Miles City and go to one of those churches, I want to see the people in it."

Van Den Heuvel nodded.

"Hmm," said Van Den Heuvel. "I wish I could join you. The Devil's work must be, to succeed, plausible enough."

"I don't think that I go there with a Jesuit," said Du Pré. "I do not want to hurt your feelings."

"Yes," said the big priest.

Du Pré rose and he left. He got in his cruiser and he went to town and gassed the car at the little grocery, laundromat, and service station, waving at the kid through the window.

Write it down, whatever it is.

Du Pré drove on. He saw the boy coming out to read the charge on the pumps.

Wednesday night.

Madelaine had said he was dumb enough to want to listen to some redneck preacher rant she would go, Mass, pray for him.

"I got cousins got sent to school run by those people," she said. "They did not do so well. Made them hate that they were Indians, those people, them evangelists, usually molested the kids, too. Pret' sick bad people. I don't like them so good."

Du Pré didn't either, but, then he never had known very many.

Me with my priests and old ones like Benetsee, like Mrs. High Back Bone, who come here and gathered herbs with my mother.

Mrs. High Back Bone was maybe Assiniboine, funny old lady, had a laugh, very warm, round fat face. Medicine person, people come to her, she cure them, cure them of broken hearts even. Cure them, stomach cancer and bad lungs.

Du Pré had been bitten by a rattlesnake and Mrs. High Back Bone had chewed some leaves and put it on the bites and Du Pré felt the poison leave his body. The paste of green leaves turned black. She washed it off and touched the wounds. The next morning Du Pré had two little white spots where the fangs had gone in. Never felt sick.

The cruiser shot along at ninety. Du Pré had a little whiskey. Driving bored him and if he was a little drunk and relaxed sometimes he could think up songs as he crossed the far empty places that Montana was mostly made of.

Some day some pissant cop is gonna bust me for drunk, Du Pré thought, damn social workers everywhere.

Du Pré crested a long hill and he hit the brakes hard. There was a tractor and a hay baler behind it wallowing from side to side on the narrow ribbon of asphalt and another car coming as fast as Du Pré had been. The rancher on the tractor tossed a beer can over his shoulder and the can bounced out from under the hay baler and Du Pré's right front tire crunched it.

The car in the other lane shot past, wheels clear out on the verge, damn near over the edge. Young cowboy in an old Cadillac.

Du Pré glanced round the baler, saw the road was clear, and in a minute he was doing eighty again and then ninety down a long perfectly clear road.

He got to Miles City at five. He found a restaurant that had a lot of men in cowboy hats in it and he ate some prime rib and had a couple glasses of whiskey in coffee cups.

"We don't have a liquor license," said the waitress. "S'pose we oughta get one?"

Du Pré laughed. He sprayed a little whiskey into his moustache.

I go there protected by the Demon Rum, there, he thought. I think that I know what I will find anyway.

At a quarter to seven Du Pré drove off to an evangelical church which advertised by printing portions of its pastor's sermons. Du Pré found the ad in the Miles City paper. The pastor thought the world's ills were the work of "godless liberals."

Du Pré found the ratty building. The sign out front held cheap plastic letters and over the 7 PM it said "EVENING SERVICE." Du Pré went in when people began to arrive. Fat women and sad-looking children, men skinny and bowed by hard work. They were dressed in cheap clothes. Du Pré took a seat in the back. The congregation, about forty people, constantly turned and looked at him.

I am maybe a little dark in the skin, be here, Du Pré thought.

The amounts of the last two collections were posted on a placard hanging in front of the pulpit.

Someone started a tape of organ music. The congregation began to sing a hymn. It was awful.

Du Pré got up and walked out.

We got poor people, Toussaint, he thought, but these are poorer people yet. They don't even got themselves.

Du Pré felt sorry for them.

But they could be plenty mean.

Du Pré drove up to the downtown of Miles City. He liked the place. Still had old bars. Still had a lot of cattle people. The Bucking Horse Sale was some party. He had not been here for it for ten years. Too many people.

But it was still the West. Not like the mountains, all yuppies and ski hills and homes built on winter range so it killed off the deer and elk. All of them drive those silly four-wheel drive things, denim seat covers. Funny boots.

Du Pré went in a big old high-ceilinged saloon and he got a drink and he walked around it looking at the pictures on the walls. Signed pictures. Tom Mix and Art Acord and Hoot Gibson. Monty Montana and Yakima Canutt. Casey Tibbs the rodeo champion. Will James, who had been born . . . what? Nepthele Dumont, something like that, French-Canadian. Drank himself to death. Du Pré's grandfather had known James, they spoke in Coyote French, though James was from Quebec.

Du Pré stopped before a little watercolor in a heavy gilt frame that was bolted to the wall.

Charley Russell. Him and Du Pré's great grandfather had been great friends, drank together till Charley quit. Charley had painted Du Pré's great-grandfather many times, the Métis with the carbine with the stock all full of brass tacks. Métis moccasins and Red River hat, sash. Charley wore a Métis sash every day of his life, even wore it with a tuxedo.

That Red River, she reach far.

Du Pré had another drink.

He went out to his cruiser and he headed back home.

I guess I just want to be with myself and think.

It was still light and Du Pré was within a hundred miles of Toussaint before it got dark enough to bother with the headlights.

He shot along.

A coyote ran in front of him and disappeared in the shadows.

Du Pré laughed.

Couple miles farther on, another.

Du Pré laughed.

Du Pré wound up a long rise that ended on a bench of stone that once must have been a tall butte.

There was a turnout at the top and Du Pré pulled over and he got out and he fished the whiskey bottle out from under the seat and he rolled a cigarette and he sat on the warm hood of his car. The night air was chilling down fast.

The coyotes suddenly started to sing. First one, then more, then a whole chorus.

Gettin' ready to hunt.

Just like Du Pré.

Du Pré howled once.

A coyote howled back.

Benetsee?

✤ CHAPTER 17 ✤

The night was black except for the silver starlight which made soft ghosts of the sage and Siberian elms that crept up to Benetsee's cabin. Du Pré turned off in the driveway and he could smell woodsmoke.

Ah, the old bastard is back. Never know where he goes, Canada, the moon, China, maybe. The fucking North Pole.

Du Pré parked by the falling-down front porch. He went to the door and he knocked.

Nothing.

He looked in the window. A kerosene lamp was burning low.

The old dogs had all finally died. Du Pré missed them, woofing and wheezing and trying to do dog work to the last, even when they could barely get up anymore.

Du Pré had tried to give Benetsee a blue heeler pup, but the old man said no, he would not live long enough and so the dog would be sad because its master would be gone.

The smell of smoke was pretty thick. Du Pré knocked again.

Nothing. He went around back to where Benetsee's sweat lodge was.

Big fire gone down to coals now, the pit where the stones were heated before being carried to the steam pit in the sweat lodge. The flaps were down on the lodge and tendrils of steam rose from the seams and curled in the night air.

In there, he is praying.

Or fucking a goat, maybe.

So I wait.

Du Pré went back to his car and he opened the trunk and rummaged around and found a bottle of the cheap awful screwtop wine that Benetsee liked so much. He carried that and his whiskey and tobacco back to the sweat lodge and he sat on a stump smoking and drinking whiskey and looking up at the stars. A green streak of fire shot across the black and it bloomed and faded in seconds.

Meteor.

Another.

Another.

Du Pré wondered why they burned with green fire, little yellow, but mostly green.

He had a slug of whiskey.

Du Pré heard some singing coming from the sweat lodge.

The lodge would be cooling and soon the old man would crawl out, wearing only his loincloth, and he would dance in the cool night air while the sweat rolled off him in streams.

Du Pré rolled a cigarette for the old fart.

I got plenty question for him, thought Du Pré.

The flap of canvas over the door shook and then a hand poked a stick up into it and opened the door all the way. Steam rose in the night air.

A young man emerged, naked, carrying a dipper.

He stopped when he saw Du Pré, reached back in the lodge and brought out a towel which he wrapped around his waist.

Du Pré waited for Benetsee.

He didn't come.

The young man stood with his arms raised to heaven, his lips moving but making no sound.

Then he went around behind the lodge and he pulled his clothes from the branches of the blue spruces and he dressed.

Du Pré smoked.

That old fucker, he thought, he is not even here.

"Good evening," said the young man, coming toward Du Pré. He was dressed in jeans and boots and a worn Western shirt. He had a belt buckle made of black metal and bear claws. A turquoise and buffalo-bone choker around his neck.

"I come to see Benetsee," said Du Pré. "Would you like some wine?"

"I don't drink anymore," said the young man. "Thank you, though."

Du Pré nodded. Res Indian here.

"Where is Benetsee?" said Du Pré.

"He gone to North Dakota," said the young man. "You are Du Pré."

"Yes," said Du Pré.

"He say you catch these guys he come back then."

"WHAT?!" said Du Pré.

"Don't yell," said the young man, "the spirits are still here, they do not like yelling. You know that."

"I got to talk to Benetsee," said Du Pré.

"Look," said the young man, "I am telling you what he told me to tell you, I don't know about nothin' else."

"Shit," said Du Pré.

"I am here to take care of his place and do . . . some things," the young man said. "I don't be telling Benetsee what he may do."

"Who," said Du Pré, "the fuck are you?"

"I don't got a name yet," the young man said. "I had one but Benetsee said it wasn't my name so I . . ."

"Christ," said Du Pré.

"Well," said the young man, "he said you'd help me I needed it."

"Yah," said Du Pré, "look, I am sorry. I am wanting to talk to that old bastard and it made me mad he was not here."

"He is not coming till you catch those guys," said the young man.

"You told me that," said Du Pré.

"I am sorry," said the young man.

"It is all right," said Du Pré. "Maybe I just kick that old fucker's ass I see him."

The young man said nothing.

"You got food," said Du Pré.

"No," said the young man, "I been fasting and praying, and Benet-see . . ."

"Come on then," said Du Pré. "My Madelaine always likes, feed people. When you eat, last time?"

"Long time ago," said the young man.

Du Pré got up from the stump. He picked up the wine and whiskey and the cigarette he had rolled for Benetsee. He stopped.

"You smoke?" he said.

"Sure," said the young man.

Du Pré lit the cigarette and gave it to him. They walked to his old cruiser and got in and they sat there a moment and then Du Pré started the engine and he drove to Toussaint and up to Madelaine's. The lights were all off.

Du Pré opened the door and went in. The young man followed him to the kitchen. Du Pré set down his whiskey bottle and he opened the refrigerator and he got out some cheese and a pot of venison stew and some green beans.

Jug of milk.

Du Pré put the stew on the stove to heat and the green beans he dumped in a pan and turned the gas on under them.

"Hey," said Madelaine from the doorway. "You are back late. Who is your friend, here?"

"Guy at Benetsee's," said Du Pré. "Hasn't eaten in days. He is very hungry."

Madelaine came out into the kitchen wearing her robe. She was rubbing her eyes against the light.

"What is your name, I am Madelaine," she said.

"I don't got a name," said the young man. "Benetsee say the name I had is no good, he will help me find another when I am ready."

"You don't got a name," said Madelaine.

"That damn Benetsee he is some joker, you know," said Du Pré. The young man nodded.

"He learn from them coyotes," said the young man. "They are jokers, them God's dogs."

"Where is Benetsee?" said Madelaine.

"He say he is not coming back till I catch those guys," said Du Pré.

"Guys?" said Madelaine.

"There are two of them," said Du Pré.

"Three," said the young man.

"Christ," said Du Pré, "I could have asked you."

"You say you want to talk, Benetsee," said the young man. "I got to learn to listen pret' good."

"Benetsee say you help me?"

The young man nodded.

"He tell you to tell me things?"

More nods.

The stew was bubbling. Du Pré took it off the stove. He stuck a ladle in it and handed the young man a bowl.

"Eat," he said.

Du Pré and Madelaine watched while the young man ate all of the stew and all of the green beans. A pound of cheese. A pint of ice cream. Drank a bunch of coffee.

Du Pré rolled him a cigarette.

They smoked.

"There are three killers?" said Du Pré.

The young man shook his head.

"Two," said the young man. "Third guy, he is . . . it is over, when they are all together."

"OK," said Du Pré.

"Good food," said the young man. "I thank you."

"You eat here plenty," said Madelaine, looking at him carefully.

"Who is there, Mama?" said Lourdes from the dark little hall that led to the bedrooms in the back of the house.

"You come here," said Madelaine. "You meet this young man got no name."

Lourdes came out of the dark.

She looked at the floor.

The young man folded his hands in his lap and his face closed up.

❧ CHAPTER 18 ❧

A gain?" said Du Pré. He was in the Toussaint bar. Agent Pidgeon was on the other end of the line. She was yelling.

"Again? Again?" she yelled. "You sexist pig asshole! What do you mean, again? Just because I'm a woman the fucking cheap-ass government surrey they give me blew up again? Fuck you, Du Pré."

"Um," said Du Pré. "I am just wondering, you know, that it blew up again."

"Fucking did," said Agent Pidgeon.

"So where are you this blown-up thing?"

"Maybe forty miles south of Toussaint."

"You calling from a ranch?"

"No," said Agent Pidgeon. "This guy stopped, he's got a phone in his van. So I am using that."

"What guy?" said Du Pré.

"He does something with the combine crews. Mechanic, I guess. Lot of fucking tools here."

"OK," said Du Pré. "I be there. You are on the highway."

"Yup," said Agent Pidgeon. "Left side of it, way you're coming."

"I be there, half an hour," said Du Pré.

"It's forty fucking miles," said Agent Pidgeon.

"Maybe less," said Du Pré.

He kept the cruiser flat out, the speed close to 120 where he could see far enough ahead.

Hope no fucking deer decides to jump out of them bushes, Du Pré thought. A magpie splattered on the windshield.

Agent Pidgeon was looking at her watch and nodding grimly when Du Pré roared up.

"Twenty-one minutes," she said. "What an asshole."

She was sitting on her suitcases. No aluminum trunks this time.

"Where is your friend?" said Du Pré.

"Simpson?" said Agent Pidgeon. "He had to go on, said he had a down rig somewhere south of here."

Du Pré shrugged. Leave a defenseless woman alone out here. Agent Pidgeon was naked but for her Sig Sauer 9mm. and God Knows What unarmed combat training she had in and out of the FBI.

Du Pré piled her luggage in the backseat. He got in and Pidgeon opened the passenger door and she slid in, and pushed her skirt back up her long thighs. Her foot clunked against a bottle.

Du Pré reached over and picked up the bottle of whiskey. He had a nice long swallow. He rolled a cigarette.

Three minutes later they were shooting along at 120 miles an hour. Agent Pidgeon was moving her mouth a lot but Du Pré couldn't hear what she was saying because of the wind rushing through the open windows and the screaming engine.

Du Pré didn't need to hear what she was saying.

He slowed down a couple miles from Toussaint and he drove on in to the bar and he got out and walked inside and left Agent Pidgeon sitting in the car calling him all of the names she could think of, which was quite a few names.

By the time that Agent Pidgeon had run down enough to get out of the car Du Pré was halfway through his second whiskey.

"I need to rent the little trailer," said Agent Pidgeon to Susan Klein. Susan had two small trailers that she rented by the day or week.

"Both rented, honey," said Susan. "Harvesttime."

"Shit," said Agent Pidgeon.

"You can stay at Bart's," said Du Pré.

"I haven't got a *car*," wailed Pidgeon.

"You would you didn't keep blowing them up," said Du Pré.

"OK," said Pidgeon. "The damsel-in-distress don't mean shit to you."

"Stay out at Bart's," said Susan. "He's a nice guy and he has a bunch of cars."

"It's against regulations," said Pidgeon.

"Oh, fuck you," said Susan.

And they all laughed.

Du Pré turned away and then he looked back at Susan, whose face had gone troubled.

Pidgeon was still laughing but it was not laughter. She began to scream.

Susan raced around the bar and she grabbed Pidgeon and held her, and the FBI agent broke down to gasping sobs and floods of tears.

Du Pré went to the phone and he called Madelaine.

Du Pré came back and Susan Klein looked at him and she jerked her head toward the row of liquor bottles ranked below the big mirror behind the bar. Du Pré went back and he pulled a fifth of brandy out and he put some in a snifter and he slid it across.

Pidgeon took the snifter in both hands. She was shaking so badly that Susan Klein was holding her on the barstool. Pidgeon lifted the glass and she took a sip. Another.

She snuffled.

Du Pré fished out his handkerchief and thought better of it and he took the box of tissues from the cupboard by the cash register and he handed it over.

Pidgeon sipped.

She slumped so deep she seemed boneless.

Madelaine came bustling through the door.

She glanced at Du Pré and then she went to Pidgeon and she hugged her and said something very low.

Pidgeon nodded.

"We take her to my place," Madelaine said. "Me and Susan, you maybe watch the bar."

Du Pré nodded. "I bring her luggage."

Madelaine and Susan led Pidgeon out the front door. In a minute, Du Pré heard them drive off.

Du Pré whistled. He washed some coffee cups and a couple of beer glasses that had tomato juice stuck to the sides.

The bar was empty.

Du Pré flicked on the television.

He poured himself a whiskey and water and he rolled a cigarette and he watched a dumb commercial for snowmobiles. In . . . July? No, July was maybe two days away.

The news came on.

The announcer, a woman with bright red hair, said that the body of a missing schoolteacher, lost since the Sunday before, had been found near Sheridan, Wyoming. The woman had been abducted, police thought, in Billings, and there was no comment to reporters' questions.

Was this the work of the Hi-Line Killer?

Oh, thought Du Pré, now they got a *name* for the bastard, next they have a TV movie.

Hi-Line Killer.

I find that fucker.

Yes.

"Du Pré?" said a soft voice at Du Pré's elbow. Du Pré started.

The young man who lived at Benetsee's was standing there.

Du Pré hadn't heard him come in.

He never heard Benetsee, either.

"Yah," said Du Pré. He was pissed. He heard *everything*.

"Your friend, the lady who is upset?" said the young man. His face was earnest and he was eager to say what he had to say.

"Yah," said Du Pré.

"Would she have some pictures of the bodies where they were found?" said the young man. "I maybe look at them, I could maybe help."

Du Pré looked at him.

Fucking little joker, I want Benetsee, not your sorry ass.

But he come from Benetsee.

Who is not coming.

"OK," said Du Pré. "I don't know when she feel well enough to see you, though."

"She is fine now," said the young man. "Look, I just walk up there."

"OK," said Du Pré. "That Madelaine, she fix you something to eat."

"I maybe take some brandy for that Pidgeon," said the young man.

Du Pré handed him the bottle.

He watched him go to the door, walking soft as a cat, his feet on a line, balanced, coiled. He slipped out, barely opening the heavy plank door.

Slipped into the light, Du Pré thought, he is here, he is not here.

I just give away Susan's brandy.

Du Pré stuffed a twenty in the till.

A couple ranchers from the benchlands came in, red and sweaty. They had several cold glasses of beer each. They went out again, arguing about the tractor being broken down and why it was.

Du Pré watched the television. He hoped to hell no one ordered a hamburger. He'd never cooked one here.

Susan Klein came in. She bustled up to the bar and around behind it.

"Pidgeon's much better," she said.

Du Pré nodded.

"She sort of lost it thinking about all the women this bastard has killed, and just before you picked her up she heard about another body found down by Sheridan. A young schoolteacher, she was only twenty-two."

Probably looked about sixteen, Du Pré thought. My age, they look sixteen until they are maybe thirty-five. Kids.

"You go on up there," said Susan. "That young Indian guy is there. He brought up some brandy."

Du Pré nodded.

"He wants to look at some pictures," said Susan Klein. "The pictures are in her stuff, there."

Du Pré took a go-cup of whiskey and a fresh bag of Bull Durham and some fried pork rinds.

Du Pré drove up to Madelaine's.

Pictures.

Young-Man-Who-Has-No-Name wanted to look at them.

I would like that, too, Du Pré thought.

❖ CHAPTER 19 ❖

The young man sat at the kitchen table. He had three large black-and-white photographs on the white enamel top.

There was a big clear glass of iced water in his hand.

The young man bent his head and he looked through the glass at the photographs. He cocked his head this way and that, like a bird, using one eye and then the other.

Du Pré and Madelaine and Pidgeon leaned against the kitchen counters. Du Pré and Pidgeon were smoking.

The young man moved to another photograph.

He stared down through the ice, water, and glass. He moved the glass in little bits of motion.

Pidgeon was red-eyed but calm. Her strong jaw was set.

They waited.

The young man kept on looking, photograph to photograph, intent and out of time.

Pidgeon jerked her head toward the door and looked at Du Pré.

He followed her out to the back porch, past the boots and coats waiting on another winter. Pidgeon opened the screen door and she went down the three steps to the yard and over to some chairs under a willow tree.

She sat down and lit a cigarette. She sucked the smoke deep into her lungs and blew out a long blue stream, eyes closed.

Du Pré took another chair and he rolled a smoke.

"Thanks," said Pidgeon.

"Yah," said Du Pré.

"I haven't lost it like that for a while. Not supposed to let this stuff get to you. It gets to you. Those poor women. They come to me in my dreams. I was raised by kind and loving parents. Ozzie 'n' Harriet kinda family, you know. I think of those poor runaway girls screaming while this bastard rapes and tortures and kills them. I hate him. I am not supposed to. Not professional."

"It don't seem very professional not give a shit," said Du Pré.

"Harvey really likes you," said Pidgeon. "Said you're one of them Montana cowboys that's more'n half-Indian. Crazy fuckers, what Harvey says, but you can trust them. He told me about . . . the Martins, and that guy Lucky . . . and how you and Bart came to be such good friends."

Du Pré shrugged.

"Tell me about Benetsee," she said.

"Him," said Du Pré, "he is an old man, been around here long as anybody. Good friend to my grandfather, my father, me. Old drunk, he is, sometimes. Dreamer. Medicine Person, holy person. Funny man, though some time he make jokes on me I want to kill him."

"He's Métis?"

"Dunno," said Du Pré. "We are all over, you know, some of us act real white, live whiteside. Some of us been doing that generations, don't even know we are Métis anymore. Some of us live on the reservations, are more Indian. Lots of us around. Whites call us Indian. Indians call us white. Catch shit, everywhere. Been like that for three hundred years. More. Some say we were here before Columbus."

"How?" said Pidgeon.

"Seapeoples," said Du Pré. "Celts, you know, Breton French, Irish, Scots, maybe sail here, their little fishing smacks, long time. Catch the cod, dry it, take it to Portugal, sell it for bacãlao. We are the voyageurs, most of the Mountain Men, they were Métis. Got French names, Scottish names, look Indian."

"What's the name of the guy with the ice water, in there?" said Agent Pidgeon.

"He don't got one," said Du Pré. "I guess he had one but Benetsee say it is the wrong one. So he is waiting for a name."

"I see," said Pidgeon. "Is he an apprentice?"

"Dunno," said Du Pré. "That Benetsee, when I say he joke, it is true. Be like that Benetsee, hide in the bushes, watch us listen to some guy don't know shit."

Pidgeon looked at him startled.

"I am being pissy," said Du Pré. "Benetsee not do that, this guy is maybe some relation of his, wants to learn from Benetsee. You can't decide to be a Medicine Person. It just happens. Happen to anybody. Happens to whites, once in a while. They see things maybe."

"Anything that will help," said Pidgeon, "will help."

Madelaine came out, carrying a little tray with three cups of coffee on it. She set it on a low-cut cottonwood stump and she took a chair that Du Pré pulled up for her.

"Him something," said Madelaine. "I don't know what he is seeing, but he is seeing something."

"He was telling me about Benetsee," said Pidgeon. "I wish that I could meet him."

"Oh." Madelaine laughed. "He will be here sometime."

Du Pré pulled out the map of the West with all the marks on it where the bodies had been found, dozens and dozens.

He unfolded it. The paper was getting beaten and soft. He carried it in his hip pocket, always. There were two more like it at Bart's.

Madelaine looked once at it and she looked away. Her lips moved a little. Hail Mary.

"First off," said Pidgeon, "this guy may have been doing this for as long as twenty years."

She was pointing to the crop of x's stippled up the Front Range of the Rockies. The old Great North Trail.

"And this one," she said, pointing to the trail that began near Puget Sound, "may have been doing this for fifteen. Ten, more likely. Hard crimes to solve. That bastard Bundy may have killed ninety women. We'll never know."

Green River Killer. Ted Bundy. Hi-Line Killer. What they call this asshole come out from Seattle?

Bastards. They die some, soon.

Du Pré was getting angry looking at it.

"They are not all him," said Du Pré. "Not all them two."

"No," said Pidgeon. "Of course not. But enough of them are. The Bureau has been on this for three years. Before that, we weren't welcome. The killer spread the damage across so many jurisdictions and we can't in law come in on this sort of thing till we're asked. Nobody asked. When they did ask—Sheriff down in southern Colorado, in fact—the crimes led both directions. Christ, what a mess. This guy knew what he was doing. He'd drop bodies in places where jurisdictions overlapped. Then nobody wanted the cases."

Madelaine got up and she took the coffee cups and she went into the house with the tray.

"I'm going to Sheridan," said Pidgeon, "soon's we wangle a request from the cops there. Could you come?"

"What I do there?" said Du Pré.

"Think," said Pidgeon.

"Take the guy in there," said Du Pré.

"Hmm," said Pidgeon. "I'll think about that."

"Me," said Du Pré, "I live here, I know here, what I can maybe do I do here. Don't want to go, you know."

Pidgeon nodded.

"What else can you tell me, maybe, about this guy," said Du Pré.

"Oh," said Pidgeon. "I don't favor getting too cute and specific. Trouble with that is that then that's what you are looking for. Profiles are pretty good up to a point. After that, they can blind you."

Pidgeon got up and went into the house.

Du Pré smoked.

The sun was warm. He looked up for the eagle but he couldn't see it, he scanned the sky for a black speck.

Nothing.

Pidgeon came back out.

"He left," said Pidgeon.

"Huh?" said Du Pré.

"Yup," said Pidgeon. "Told Madelaine that the little girl was the work of one man and that the other three were the work of another."

Du Pré nodded.

"That there is witchcraft around the killer of the little girl."

Witchcraft? What the fuck he mean by that? Du Pré thought, we got green-skinned hags boiling up lizards here? Witchcraft.

"You're going to Sheridan," said Pidgeon.

OK, thought Du Pré, my Madelaine is in this.

"Day after tomorrow, I guess."

Du Pré nodded.

"Bart's flying us down and back," said Pidgeon.

My Madelaine she has been on the telephone. World is cranking around all right, she has seen to it.

"That OK," said Pidgeon, "with you?"

Du Pré nodded.

"Good," said Pidgeon. "I guess I'll be staying here."

Du Pré nodded.

"Du Pré!" Madelaine yelled through the kitchen window. "You got a phone call here!"

Du Pré got up and he went to the steps and he tripped and fell going up, catching himself on the jamb.

Madelaine was looking sad.

She handed him the phone.

"Du Pré?" said Benny Klein.

"Yah," said Du Pré.

"Another."

"Shit. Where are you."

"Blaine's Cut."

Years ago some crazy old man had cut a road through rock.

Charged a quarter to use it. The only way to get up to the top of a dry riverbed, left over from when the glaciers melted.

And then up into the Wolf Mountains, so the miners paid.

It was maybe fifteen miles away.

Right next to Bart's land.

"I be there," said Du Pré.

Pidgeon was sitting in his cruiser when he got there.

♣ CHAPTER 20 ♣

Now I spend the rest of my life looking at crosses in the earth and remembering, Du Pré thought. I ever find this guy I kill him what he has done to what I see every day.

Du Pré was about six feet up the left wall of Blaine's Cut, looking at what at first glance seemed to be a tree root sticking out of a wide cleft in the fragile rock. It was a human foot, with dark brown skin, dried and mummified. The toenails were dark yellow-brown.

There was a vertical cut in the rock about ten feet to Du Pré's right. Left arm of the cross, right hand of Christ.

Du Pré looked in the cleft. He squinted. The body had been in a duffel bag. The canvas had rotted and the edges of the tears were white. Insects crawled over the dried corpse. It didn't look like anything human.

Du Pré dropped back down to the ground.

"No telling how long that's been there," said Benny.

"Years," said Pidgeon. "Who found it?"

"Kid out shooting his .22," said Benny. "Shot at the foot. Toenail fell off. Smart kid. He took one look at the toenail and he ran like hell. Got his dad and the old man come and crawled up there and then he called me. No telling how many people just walked right by this, you know."

"I dunno how I'll get the body out of there," said Benny.

"You'll have to hook it out," said Pidgeon, "and it'll probably break up. Pretty dry and brittle. Where's the toenail?"

Benny handed her a glassine envelope. Pidgeon looked at it for a long time.

"Got a little red polish on it," said Pidgeon.

Du Pré nodded.

Pidgeon was looking up at the top of the cut. The sagebrush hung over the sheer edge a little. She made a clicking sound with her tongue.

"What's up there?" said Pidgeon.

Du Pré nodded and he started up the cut so he could get up top and look. Pidgeon was wearing lady penny loafers with little gold chains over the arch of the foot.

Du Pré found a steep path that cut back and forth twice in rising ten feet to the top of the limestone shelf. He went up it. He had to grab a sagebrush at the top and hoist himself over the crumbling lip of yellow-gray rock and earth.

Du Pré looked off to the west. A rutted track looped and meandered back and forth through the dry tough benchland, one that avoided the rocks that stuck up high enough to grab a transmission. Grass grew in the ruts. Sparse yellow blades. They had been flattened. Someone had driven up here recently. He walked back along the lip toward the vertical cleft that split the formation.

Water. Du Pré rolled a smoke. Water and mountains fight, water it always win. Takes a long time, though. People, we don't got that much time. Old stories.

Du Pré stood and thought of dead women lying alone in the dirt, eyes pecked out by birds, skunks chewing their faces.

He went to the cleft and he looked down. Pidgeon and Benny were looking up at him.

Du Pré glanced around.

"No more bodies up here," he said, spreading his hands, palms up.

Benny called him a son of a bitch.

This is not funny, Benny, thought Du Pré. No, it is not funny.

One spur of the rutted track came to within fifty feet of Du Pré. He walked over to it, a circle wide enough for a pickup truck to turn around in. He walked around it slowly. Couple old beer cans. Deer hunters, antelope hunters. Du Pré glanced up. A half dozen antelope were running up the long slope of the next short hill.

Them prairie scooters. Move some. Good meat.

Du Pré stopped and he breathed deeply and he set his mind to lock out sounds and the wind and all that was not in his first sight. To bring the ground up to his eyes, see what was on it that shouldn't be there.

At the place he had begun, when he returned to it after a time spent walking slowly, he glanced toward the center of the loop and he saw something circular.

No circles out here but eyes.

Du Pré walked over to the small circle in the yellow earth. He bent down and he looked a long time.

Socket. From a socket wrench set. Expensive kind, that black metal. Little yellow mud on the top, hard to see.

Du Pré rubbed the dirt from the outside of the socket.

9/16.

Made in America.

Snap-On Tool Corporation.

Du Pré had seen their trucks. They went around to where mechanics worked and they had a huge assortment of tools. Gave credit till payday.

9/16.

Du Pré put the socket in his pocket and he went back to the lip of the cut and he looked down at Pidgeon and Benny.

"Nothing here much," said Du Pré.

Socket probably rolled out of somebody's pickup they open the door. That is how I lose mine. When I figure out how I lose my sunglasses, I will be better, you bet.

Du Pré walked back down to the narrow steep path and he dropped off the edge and he landed and flexed his knees to absorb the shock and he took tiny steps quickly till he was at the bottom and could lengthen his stride.

"Had some maybe antelope hunters, deer hunters up there," he said, "Beer cans. Found this, it maybe roll out of somebody's truck."

Du Pré handed the socket to Pidgeon.

She looked at it and nodded.

"Shit," said Benny. "I have lost more a them damn things, you know, the box bounces open and they fly out and roll out the door

96

when you open it. And there goes another three, four bucks. For the good ones, anyway."

"This is a professional's tool?" said Pidgeon.

"Yah," said Du Pré. "But you got, remember, all the ranchers here have to be pret' good mechanics, pret' good welders, pret' good carpenters, all them things . . ."

"Pretty good psychics, too," said Benny, "and gamblers. Cattle business is like a damn séance. Always has been, I guess, when you deal in live things you never know what's going to happen."

"OK," said Pidgeon. "Now, you gonna drag the bones out of the rocks, there?"

Benny nodded miserably.

"I do it," said Du Pré. "You got a something I can use?"

Benny went to his truck and he got a boathook out and a black body bag. He brought them back.

"I got a ladder, too," he said.

He fetched it.

Du Pré put the ladder up against the rock, to the left of the dried corpse jammed in the horizontal cleft. He went up the ladder and he picked up the boathook and he reached in and jiggled the hook for a purchase and he pulled.

The whole bundle moved, and very easily.

Du Pré inched it toward him.

Smell of stale old corruption. Some startled mice scurried off from their nests under the rotted canvas bag.

Du Pré got the bundle out to the edge of the rock face. He dropped the boathook and he grasped the bundle and he slid it forward and let it fall.

He squinted and looked in.

Couple lumps of something there.

"Benny!" said Du Pré. "You hand me that boathook again, maybe?"

Benny did.

Du Pré pulled and scraped the lumps out.

Looked like old hide, all balled up.

One lump had some brown hair on it, fairly long.

An ear.

Christ, Du Pré thought, this is the skin of her *face*.

Du Pré dropped it over the side. And another brown gob.

He looked in. The rock floor of the cleft was clean. There were stains, dark ones, where the bundle had sat.

I wonder how that foot got out there.

Skunk shit there, a foot from my nose, all dried and black.

Coyotes could make it in here, too.

They chew and drag. Wonder they did not drag the whole thing off.

Du Pré went down the ladder. Benny was zipping up the black body bag. He carried it to his truck. Du Pré followed with the ladder and the boathook.

"Where," said Pidgeon, "in the name of God did you find a boathook in this fucking desert?"

"Navy recruiter," said Benny, solemnly. "Busted him for speeding. He didn't have any money, so the judge took this."

He is some better, now, thought Du Pré!

"Thanks," said Benny.

"You send that to Helena?" said Du Pré.

"I drive it to Helena," said Benny.

Du Pré nodded.

"The north–south guy," said Pidgeon.

Du Pré nodded.

❖ CHAPTER 21 ❖

Du Pré drove into Toussaint past combine crews harvesting the hard red wheat. The giant machines marched slowly across the golden fields, trucks grinding along beside them, receiving thick streams of hulled grain. One combine, two trucks. When one truck was full it would pull ahead, the second would move up under the spout, and the first would head for the metal storage bins standing at the ranch houses.

Lotta damn noodles, Du Pré thought, wish I liked noodles better.

He drove into the little town and to the bar. He parked and walked inside. There were a lot of strangers in the bar, drinking beers and eating and playing the video poker machines.

The combines ran twenty-four hours when the weather was good. All night, with giant spotlights hung on the cabs focused on the wheat. The whole year's work on the fields brought in, the bank's notes paid off. Everyone hoped. Maybe something left over. Wheat was up.

The off-duty crews were using part of their twelve-hour break to let off a little steam. They talked in soft Texas accents. They had started down in Texas three months before, working their way north with the ripening grain.

The pool table was busy. Quarters piled beside the coin slot. The players waited. Money was bet on these games, and on the poker games that went on round the clock, too.

Boomers. Make it, spend it right away.

Du Pré grinned. He liked these people.

They never caused much trouble, and anyway they would never fight in a bar. They needed that bar, and being 86'd from it would make life very hard indeed. They fought across the street in the parking lot.

Susan Klein was scurrying fast behind the bar, drawing beers, mixing drinks, and somehow getting hamburgers and french fries done right and on plates.

She got a good timer in her head, Du Pré thought. He went round the bar and he made himself a whiskey ditch and he dropped a twenty on the ledge of the cash register.

The owners of the equipment sat at corner tables, writing checks, lending money to crew members till payday, and then they'd leave a day or two ahead of the crews, on to the next place of work, and see to all arrangements. The owners were weathered men in their sixties, in light straw cowboy hats and custom boots with lone stars on the front of them.

Susan caught up for a moment. She ran a couple of bar napkins across her forehead. The place was hot. The day was hot and there were a lot of people there and the grill was going.

"Looks good," said Susan. "If the weather lasts another week, the wheat will be in. No problems."

Other years, it had rained, and the grain had to wait for the sun. Put up damp, it would mold. Running grain dryers was expensive. There weren't enough of them. Not needed until they were needed, and then too much grain for the ones at hand.

The big parking lot across the street was filled with the motor homes that the crews lived in. In past years, the ranchers put the crews up in bunkhouses, but since farm and ranch hands had been replaced pretty much by machinery, the bunkhouses had rotted or burned down.

Combine gypsies.

Voyageurs.

Du Pré sipped his drink.

"Could you maybe do some music tonight?" said Susan. "Crews switch at nine or ten, so if you started at seven or so then both shifts could hear you."

Du Pré nodded.

"Thanks," said Susan.

Du Pré thought about who he could get to back him up.

Couple kids. Ranch kids, one played pretty good rhythm guitar and the other pretty good bass.

Wish my cousins were here, they got some music in them.

The kids are OK, just too young.

And they like the old songs. Guitar player he wants to fiddle, I give him one lesson, a tape of simple stuff, say, when you can do all this perfectly then I give you another. Me, I don't listen to you practice at all. I listen to myself practice is bad enough.

Du Pré called the boys, who weren't in but their mothers said they thought they would, which meant that they would.

These ranch women pret' tough.

Du Pré laughed.

A young man in faded denims and worn boots and a battered hat yee-hawed. Du Pré glanced at the point register at the top of the video poker machine's screen. Past five hundred and climbing, so the kid had hit a Royal Flush, Ordered. Ten to ace, left to right. That was eight hundred bucks.

Susan laughed and she went in the back to get the money. The young man brought the slip of paper to the bar and he waited, grinning.

Susan glanced at the little slip of paper. She handed over the eight hundred-dollar bills.

"Drinks for the house!" the young man yelled.

Everybody whooped, even Du Pré.

"Buy me a few new clothes and get my truck some new tires," said the young cowboy. "Then I'll put ten times this back into them damn machines figuring I am going to win big again. You don't, I know, but it is some way to pass the time."

Du Pré glanced at his hand. Wedding band. He was a long way from his wife. Probably missed her a lot.

Du Pré went out and he drove up to Madelaine's. She was in the kitchen, kneading bread dough. Wednesday. Baking day. Madelaine had a baking day, two cleaning days, two sewing days, a day to relax, and one day she prayed more or less all day. Unless she went to bed with Du Pré, or he offered to buy her pink wine and dance to the music on the jukebox with her.

She liked that two-step.

No Métis music, that. She danced the reels and clogs, too, but she really liked the two-step. Liked Nashville music. Cheating hearts, drunks, trucks, prison, railroad trains.

Her father had worked all of his life on the Great Northern Railroad, even though it wasn't called that any more after Burlington bought it.

Line that Jim Hill built, Du Pré thought, then the Catholics, they buy railroad cars that are chapels, run them on to a siding, say to the Métis, hey, François and Helene, you come get married by a priest, you bring your twelve children to watch.

Métis who come down here after Red River Rebellion, they don't talk to priests much. Priests betray Louis Riel, so the English hang him. Little Gabriel Dumont, Louis Riel's little general, brother to my great-great-grandfather, he come down here and he die fifty years later he still had not once talked to a priest. Wouldn't be buried in Catholic earth, either.

Red River.

"I play some music tonight," said Du Pré.

"Good," said Madelaine. "I be your . . . what . . . gropey?"

"Huh?" said Du Pré.

"Gropey," said Madelaine. "One them women follow musicians around, you know, want to fuck them."

"Oh," said Du Pré. "I got ten, twelve, more of them. You just be my Madelaine."

Madelaine looked at Du Pré. She smiled. She pegged a big lump of sticky dough at him. Missed. Hit St. Francis on the wall behind Du Pré.

"Damn," said Madelaine. "What kind of man are you, not save that poor saint? Damn. Poor St. Francis."

Du Pré laughed.

That evening it was still hot at six-thirty. Du Pré got into his cruiser and he drove down to the bar and he went in. Benny was setting up the little stage.

The two kids showed up, all scrubbed and eager. They were so young that they really couldn't legally play in the bar, if anyone cared to think about it.

Good kids, Du Pré thought, they never make much musicians, but they want to a lot.

News that Du Pré was playing his fiddle always brought some people down to the bar. Not so many this night, because everyone was working so hard. But there were fifty people in the room when Du Pré and his sidemen started. The harvest crews listened respectfully.

Susan Klein shut down the pool table when Du Pré played. No arguments.

Madelaine came in after nine.

The night crews went out and the day crews straggled in, dusty and hot and tired and covered in bits of wheat hulls. They perked up after a lot of beer and some food.

Du Pré played some reels and some jigs.

People danced, some of them pretty well.

A couple of the Texans were really good.

Du Pré took a break after a long hour.

He bought Madelaine some pink wine.

"Everbody they think they make out pret' good this year," said Madelaine.

Du Pré nodded. Everybody always hoped that it would be a good year, wheat's up, no rain at harvesttime.

After Du Pré quit he and Madelaine danced to the jukebox. Late, till the bar closed.

✦ CHAPTER 22 ✦

Christ," yelled Pidgeon. "Do you have to drive like this?"
Du Pré laughed. The countryside was shooting by very rapidly. They were north of the Yellowstone River and south of the Missouri. The Big Dry. Where the last wild buffalo in America were slaughtered by a Smithsonian expedition.

Du Pré's great-grandfather had watched from a nearby butte.

The expedition moved on and Du Pré's grandpère had butchered out the three cows and he had smoked the meat and taken it back to his family. It was the last of the buffalo for the Métis.

Beef is pret' good, though, Du Pré thought.

"You *fucker*," yelled Pidgeon.

Du Pré looked over and he grinned.

"Drive that fifty-five you never get anywhere," said Du Pré, at the top of his lungs. "Big place, this Montana."

Pidgeon tried to light a cigarette but she couldn't get the flame on her butane lighter to keep going long enough to do it. Du Pré took the cigarette from her and he lit it with his old Zippo and handed it back.

Pidgeon smoked and looked out the window.

Du Pré slowed down to eighty-five to humor her.

"How fast were we going?" she said.

"About right," said Du Pré. From the bench he could see the Interstate along the south bank of the Yellowstone River. It was heavy with traffic and it looked very busy in the calm and empty landscape.

They crossed over the river and went up an on-ramp and headed west.

South at Hardin, on the Crow Reservation, headed for Sheridan.

Du Pré drove at sixty-five. You could drive like hell on the two-lane but the superhighways were heavily patrolled.

This schoolteacher, she was from Billings.

Dumped near Sheridan.

Missing for two days.

First one we got that's fairly fresh, Du Pré thought.

He's around.

I find him.

"I think we'll get some cooperation," said Pidgeon, "but you never know. The Bureau didn't try to spare anyone's feelings till recently."

No shit, thought Du Pré.

"So I talked to the Sheriff and he's meeting us at the Denny's at the north exit into the town."

Du Pré nodded.

Find your way around America by hamburger.

Bad hamburgers, too.

They came to the exit for the Little Bighorn Battlefield. Eleven

Métis, they die there. That Mitch Bouyer, he is leading the scouts, he try to send his friends away. He knows how many Sioux, Cheyenne, all them Plains people are down there.

Custer sends his favorite Crow scout, Half Yellow Face, away.

Mitch, he die there. Lonesome Charley Reynolds, the old trapper, he die there, too.

That Custer, he is a bastard.

Them Indian, they have their Day of Greasy Grass.

"My heart has quit pounding," said Pidgeon. "You can speed up now. I know it hurts you to obey the law."

"Me," said Du Pré, "I obey all them good laws."

"Right," said Pidgeon.

She was dressed in jeans and hiking boots and a cotton shirt and a photographer's vest. Her gun, ID, handcuffs, and such were in the pockets. She carried a camera and many rolls of film. Little tape recorder.

"There have been three other bodies left near Sheridan in the last ten years," said Pidgeon, "all young women, all mutilated, none identified. All of them treated as isolated cases. Since they were dumped years apart, I suppose."

"Me," said Du Pré, "I never know that so much of this happens."

Pidgeon nodded.

"I got into this," she said, "because of a term paper. How many women were killed and dumped and no one ever charged in their murders. Over the last twenty years, there have been thousands. *Thousands*. I couldn't believe it."

"Pret' hard to find, people who do it," said Du Pré. "They are not part of any place. Come in, kidnap someone, kill them, leave them somewhere else. Don't go back. Or kill them poor whores. They got to get in cars with men. Can't attract too much attention, cops bust them."

"These are young girls mostly," said Pidgeon, "of lower-class origin. I have heard them called trailer trash. Money's pretty damned important in this country."

Du Pré nodded. Pretty important everywhere.

"Was Bart pissed when you said you didn't want to take the offer of a plane from him?" said Pidgeon.

"No," said Du Pré, "I am trying to help him, he is too generous, some people take him for much money. He wants to help, he is a rich boy, I want him to know I like him even though he has got a lot of money."

Pidgeon snorted.

"He is a good guy."

"I like him," said Pidgeon. "He has such a sad, sweet face. A middle-aged boy who is sort of bewildered by all the trouble the world causes itself and him personally."

"Yah," said Du Pré.

They rode silently the rest of the way to Sheridan. Du Pré got off at the first exit. He could see the Denny's sign from the highway.

"We're early," said Pidgeon.

Du Pré parked the cruiser. He took off his hat and wiped his forehead and he rubbed his eyes and he yawned.

He leaned back for a moment, eyes shut.

"Hey, Du Pré," said Pidgeon. "Guess what? The Denny's is being robbed. Hey, hey."

Du Pré sat upright in a hurry.

"No sudden movements," said Pidgeon. "That car, across from the door out in the street? The one that is running? With the kid at the wheel who is smoking like hell and staring at the front door. And I notice that though Denny's is open and there are cars in the lot, I can't see anybody in there. Bet they are all lying on the floor."

Du Pré looked. Nobody was stirring in there.

"What you going to do?" said Du Pré.

"Have fun," said Pidgeon. "It's important in life, you know, to have fun. Real important. Most folks don't."

This Pidgeon, she reminds me some of that poor Corey Banning, thought Du Pré. FBI lady poor Packy killed. Some shit, that. Wolves. Balls.

Pidgeon had slid her gun out of its pocket.

She lit a cigarette.

106

"Oh," said Pidgeon. "Tell you what. It is so against every Bureau regulation, do what I would like to do, that I'm gonna let *you* do it. Here." She racked the slide and handed the Sig Sauer to Du Pré.

"What I don't like to?" said Du Pré.

"I'll tell Madelaine you wussed out," said Pidgeon. "Oh, don't kill anybody."

"OK," said Du Pré. He got out and he tucked the automatic in his waistband at his back. He walked across the little parking lot and down to the sidewalk beyond the decorative planting. The kid in the car glanced at him. Just a cowboy.

The kid went back to staring at the front door of the Denny's.

Du Pré crossed the sidewalk and he went in front of the car and he stepped out into the traffic lane.

When a truck passed, Du Pré sprinted.

He walked up to the open driver's window and he squatted down and put the barrel of the gun against the kid's head.

"Don' move," said Du Pré.

The kid shuddered.

Du Pré reached in the window and he turned off the car and pulled the keys out of the ignition and he stuck them in his pocket. He was out of sight, behind the driver.

"How many friends you got in there," said Du Pré, jamming the gun against the kid's head.

"Two," whispered the kid.

"OK," said Du Pré. "What guns they got?"

"Couple pistols. Twenty-twos."

"That's very good," said Du Pré.

Two young men came flying out of the Denny's doors. They were each carrying paper sacks in one hand and little Saturday Night Specials in the other. They ran like hell for the car.

When they were twenty feet away Du Pré stood up and he fired one round into the sky.

"Down on the ground," he said, lowering the gun.

One kid froze. The other stumbled and tripped and he went face-first into the side of the car.

Crump.

The other kid dropped the sack and his gun and he put his hands on the top of his head.

Du Pré opened the driver's door.

"You get out now," he said.

The kid did.

Du Pré prodded him around to the sidewalk. The kid who had hit the car was on his knees, holding his face, and blood welled between his hands.

Du Pré heard a siren.

Two cop cars came, lights flashing.

The cops screeched to a stop.

Du Pré waited, gun on the three young men.

❧ CHAPTER 23 ❧

Oh, this is good," said the Sheriff. He was a big, paunchy man with silver hair brushed back and squinted blue eyes.

Du Pré and Pidgeon were standing with him in the Denny's parking lot. The thugs were on their way to the jail.

The manager was being carted away in an ambulance. He'd been so scared he'd had a heart attack.

The people in the restaurant were all over the parking lot jabbering at each other.

"Well, thanks," said the Sheriff. "We know these boys. Two of them got out of the State Pen last week. Guess they weren't ree-habilitated."

He spat the word.

Cops know better.

"They were not very good at it," said Du Pré.

The Sheriff looked at Du Pré. "Most of these assholes got IQs lower'n room temperature," he said. "They ain't rocket scientists. Once in a while there's a bad guy has a brain but I don't see many. 'Bout two in the last ten years, you don't count the forgers and scam artists. Holdup guys and burglars ain't too swift."

Pidgeon was standing with them. She had on big aviator sunglasses with very dark lenses.

"We're being rude, ma'am," said the Sheriff suddenly. "I apologize."

"Not at all," said Pidgeon. "Could we go somewhere and talk, though? I have to fly out of Billings late tonight."

"Surely," said the Sheriff. "There's a saloon a couple blocks away has decent food and no jukebox. How's that?"

He drove them to it. A simple old brick building with MINT CLUB on a sign and no beer neon in the windows. The place was clean and old and a little shabby. Several old ranchers sat at the bar drinking red beers and chatting.

The Sheriff led them to a little back room with one banquette and one table in it. He threw his hat on the table and slid in one side of the banquette.

The barmaid came in.

"What'll you have?" said the Sheriff.

"Cheeseburger," said Pidgeon, "glass of soda."

Du Pré and the Sheriff ordered fries with theirs.

"I don't know that I can tell you much," said the Sheriff. "I mean I don't know more'n the skinny little ME's report and a bit about the site."

"Can you fax the full reports to me in DC?" said Pidgeon.

"Sure," said the Sheriff. "When I get 'em."

Pidgeon gave him a card.

"Well," said the Sheriff. "Poor Susannah Granger. She taught typing and some home economics at the school in Billings. It was her first year. She graduated from Bozeman, Montana State. Strict Christian. Didn't drink or smoke or run around. She had alcohol in her system, she was strangled to unconsciousness and then had her jugular cut, very carefully. The killer left her in the brush, legs splayed and a . . . uh."

"She had something shoved up her vagina or anus?" said Pidgeon.

"A stick up each one," said the Sheriff.

Pidgeon nodded. The little tape recorder sat there in front of her.

Their food arrived. Pidgeon picked at her cheeseburger.

Du Pré and the Sheriff ate like pigs.

"So you wanted to see where the body was found?" said the Sheriff.

"Changed my mind," said Pidgeon. "Du Pré and me, we need to go on to Billings."

Du Pré shrugged.

The Sheriff drove them back to Du Pré's car.

"I'd like copies of the photos of the scene," said Pidgeon. "How was the body found?"

"Pilot," said the Sheriff. "He was just logging some hours for his license and he looked down and saw her."

Du Pré wheeled back out to the expressway and he headed north.

"This is the first one that is fresh and not a young kid who is just in some sort of trouble," said Pidgeon. "The bastard's losing it."

"OK," said Du Pré.

"When a killer's pattern changes, even slightly, there is something going on with them. There's something in Billings. Something else. Susannah lived with an aunt."

They rode on to Billings. When they got there Pidgeon made several calls from a phone booth. She came back to the car with a map in her hand.

"She'll see us," said Pidgeon.

She read the directions to Du Pré. They ended at a trailer court. The trailers were neatly kept, and most had little redwood decks built on the back sides.

"Number twenty-eight," said Pidgeon. "That's it, where that blue car with the abortion-is-murder bumper sticker is."

Du Pré pulled in behind it.

"Wait here," said Pidgeon. "You'd just scare her."

Pidgeon got out and she went to the front door and knocked. The door opened. Du Pré saw a fat woman in a pantsuit. A blue one. Pidgeon went inside.

Du Pré rolled a smoke. He reached under the seat and he found his whiskey and he had a good long drink. It was getting late. He was hungry. He had some more whiskey.

He looked across the drive. There was a little compact car sitting there. Blue. It wasn't in any parking space by any trailer.

Woman must have a kid or something, Du Pré thought. It was closest to the trailer owned by the murdered woman's aunt.

Du Pré had another cigarette.

He waited another half hour before Pidgeon came back. She was excited.

"OK," she said. "Susannah was at a prayer meeting the night she was taken. After the meeting she did the church's books—so it was past midnight when she left for home. Never got here. Then, this morning the police call and say they have her car, it was abandoned about a mile from here. Off on the side of the stem road. Not much traffic there at that time of night. There aren't any fast-food places around. The stem road isn't a main drag, you can get into or across town faster other ways. So they towed it here."

Du Pré looked at the little compact car.

"OK," he said. "So what we do."

"I want to see if that car starts," said Pidgeon.

She held up a key.

Du Pré took it and he went over and got in and stuck the key in the ignition and he turned it and the starter motor turned over but the engine didn't catch. He looked at the fuel gauge. Dead empty.

No gas.

Susannah Granger had pulled over because her little car was out of gas. It was dark.

And somebody came along.

"Where this car when it was found?" said Du Pré.

"Dunno," said Pidgeon, "but I can call and find out. I've talked to the cop handled the case here."

Du Pré drove back out to the stem road and found a telephone booth.

Pidgeon was on the phone for ten minutes.

Du Pré had a smoke and some more whiskey.

"OK," said Pidgeon. "I got to get to the airport but I want you to find where the hell this place is, Spurgin Road."

"We are on it," said Du Pré.

"Oh," said Pidgeon.

"What is the number?"

"One seven five four five," said Pidgeon.

"It is about a half mile toward the airport," said Du Pré.

When they got to the place, Du Pré pointed it out. A dirt parking lot in front of a long metal building.

WELDING SUPPLIES.

OK.

So she was coming home, he thought, and she pulled off there when she ran out of gas.

Du Pré went on, up to the rimrocks above the city, to the airport.

He helped Pidgeon carry her luggage in and check it.

"Thanks, Du Pré," she said. She kissed him on the cheek.

"You come back," he said.

"You find those pricks," said Pidgeon. "You know how to get ahold of me. Or Harvey."

"You tell Harvey hello," said Du Pré. "Maybe he come out, we go hunt or something."

"Harvey hates the great outdoors," said Pidgeon. "He'll go out in it, but not for fun."

Du Pré laughed.

"But I will," said Pidgeon. "You give my love to Madelaine."

Du Pré nodded. Pidgeon went on up to the departure lounge.

He drove back down to where the car had been found. It was dark now. He got out of his cruiser and he switched on a powerful flashlight. He scanned the ground where a car might have rolled to a stop with no power.

It had rained here, three, four days before. Old mud puddles, dried now. Du Pré saw a piece of paper stuck in pale clay.

Folded many times.

Du Pré tugged it free.

FREE WILL EVANGELICAL CHURCH

A printed service.

Du Pré opened the pamphlet and he looked at the second page. He walked over toward his car and held the program in the headlights.

"solo . . . Susannah Granger . . ."

So she was a singer. In the church.

Wouldn't sing for God no more.

✤ CHAPTER 24 ✤

Du Pré sat on the hood of his car. It was four in the morning. He was up on the Hi-Line at Raster Creek, waiting for Rolly Challis. Who said he would be there at four-fifteen.

Du Pré rolled a smoke.

Guy drives this road so much he knows to the minute where he will be anywhere along it, Du Pré thought.

Looking for whoever killed little Shelly Challis.

Du Pré had some coffee from a steel thermos.

He glanced at his watch.

He heard the thrummm of Rolly's big black eighteen-wheeler.

Du Pré was looking at the second hand on his watch when Rolly came to a stop and hit the air brakes to hold the rig.

A minute early.

Damn.

Rolly stepped down from the cab. He walked on the balls of his feet, stretching his arms and back.

"Lo, Du Pré," he said. He held out his hand.

"Yah," said Du Pré. "Well, I don't see the papers much. Your guy he doing any good work out there, eh?"

"Maybe," said Rolly, "but nothing's turned up. Guy dumps the bodies in places where they are found by accident. I guess that there are some more. Real hell for the families, was for ours."

Du Pré waved the steel thermos.

Rolly shook his head.

"We had another down, Sheridan," said Du Pré.

Rolly nodded.

"You know about it," said Du Pré.

"Yeah," said Rolly. "Schoolteacher, young. Saw a picture, not an attractive young woman. Christer."

"Yeah," said Du Pré. "Fundamentalist. But she is maybe older than most this guy kills on the old Great North Trail."

"We got two. Well, I want 'em both," said Rolly. "Hard to find, though. Thought I might be getting close, case in eastern Washington, but it turned out the girl was raped and murdered by her uncle."

Jesus, Du Pré thought.

Well, there is that damn Bucky Dassault, now that Benjamin Medicine Eagle. Never murdered anybody, though. I hate him anyway.

They smoked.

"I call him the Gatherer," said Rolly. "He . . . it seems that he picks a place and then in a matter of a month or so he'll kill four, five, maybe more, and leave them hidden there, and then move on. Prostitutes. Runaway kids trying to survive. Woman's always got her Universal Credit Card . . . sometimes end up dead."

Du Pré nodded. Poor Lourdes. She was always such a sad kid. She always was unhappy. Madelaine tried what she knew, make Lourdes happy.

Nobody can make anybody happy.

Who refuses to be happy.

Me, I sound like them bullshit therapists, TV.

I quit watching TV.

There.

"I'll be along, then," said Rolly. "Thing I guess we'd better do is not quit."

They shook hands.

Du Pré drank coffee and smoked. The dawn was blood pink in the east.

Traffic started to move. A few big trucks, then the huge wallowing motor homes and the cars of people headed east or west.

Du Pré got into his old cruiser and he started it and he wheeled around the rest-stop parking lot and he headed back down south toward Toussaint.

The air was dry and cool.

Mule deer moved from their watering holes to where they would lie up in the day's head. The bucks had horns covered in velvet. Antelope flashed their white butts and sped away from the road at fifty miles an hour. The hawks cruised low, looking for rodents out too late in the light. A badger waddled across the road, steely muscles bunched and close to the ground.

Du Pré cruised at ninety.

There was no one at all on the road.

Soon he could see the Wolf Mountains whitecapped and dark-flanked in the rising light. The snow on the peaks blazed pale pink and gold.

Du Pré shot past a marsh and ducks exploded skyward.

The road rose before him, climbing a long slope.

He smelled something hot.

A steamy billow of scent came through the vents.

Du Pré glanced in the rearview mirror. He was trailing white steam.

He put the transmission in neutral and he turned off the ignition.

Now that damn engine heat up and seize, if it is gonna do that.

Only got two hundred thousand miles on it.

Piece of Detroit shit, anyway.

115

Du Pré waited for the bass clunk that would mean the engine was eating itself.

It didn't come.

He rolled to a stop, pulling off on a field access road, barely fifteen feet across.

An eighteen-wheeler roared past, close enough to rock the old cruiser on its springs.

Shit, Du Pré thought.

I hate these damn cars. I like horses. Things get tough, you can always eat your horse.

Maybe I eat this fucker. Pound of chopped steel a day, wash it down with whiskey. Maybe pound three times a day. Eat it, a year maybe.

Fucker.

A motor home sailed past. A dachshund was sticking its head out a window. The nasty little dog yapped.

Du Pré dragged the fifth of whiskey out from under the seat.

Go find a telephone, call that Bart. He can borrow Morris's tow truck, come get me.

I hate this.

Du Pré drank savagely.

Several vans with Minnesota plates shot past. They were driving close together. Take a vacation in a mob.

Du Pré had another slug. He tucked the bottle back under the seat and he rolled a smoke and got out and looked down the road.

Nothing.

Hang out my damn thumb. Me, I always look like some train robber or cattle thief. Me, I wouldn't pick up me.

Shit.

Du Pré got out and he waited to lift his thumb.

He heard a car behind him slow down.

A dark green longbed van with deeply tinted windows came to a stop across the road, on another access path.

The driver's door opened and a man got out. He was wearing mechanic's overalls. He was weathered red. Sandy, curly hair, going bald on top.

116

"Little trouble, there?" he said, walking across the road. "Name's Simpson."

"Me, Du Pré. I blew out a hose," said Du Pré. They shook hands.

"Let me take a look," the man said. "I work on cars a lot. Old cop cruiser. Plymouth. Good engine."

Du Pré shrugged. He popped the hood latch and he lifted the hood and stuck the jackleg in the socket.

Soaking steam rose up for a moment. The air reeked of antifreeze.

The man bent over and looked. He took out a pocketknife and he cut the blown hose away near the engine and he reached in the end of the hose and jiggled his forefinger.

"OK," he said. "Just a minute. . . ."

He grimaced a little, then pulled.

"Got a little piece of gasket, jammed your thermostat," he said. "You probably are OK. Didn't seize?"

"Didn't hear anything," said Du Pré.

"I got a hose'll fit that," said the man. "Got some coolant, too."

In five minutes the cruiser was purring. The man was fiddling with the adjustment on the carburetor.

"I pay you?" said Du Pré.

The man shrugged.

"Don't have to," he said. "The Lord tells us to succor the traveler."

Du Pré handed him forty dollars.

"I want to, give you this," said Du Pré. "Them hose, antifreeze cost some money, you have to replace them. You in Toussaint, I buy you a drink."

"I am near there," the man said. "I work on the combines and the trucks. Got to keep everything running. If the combines aren't working, the threshers lose money."

"You got a garage?" said Du Pré.

"Oh, no," said the man. "I have what I need in the van. I repair them right in the fields. Oh, once in a great while a whole engine will blow and that's more than I can manage, but not often. Last time was six years ago."

Du Pré nodded.

"Well," said the man, "I better go. Got a call up a ways here."

He walked across the road and got in the van and he pulled out and went down the road to the north.

Du Pré drove south, at ninety. The engine was running very well.

Pretty lucky, there, Du Pré thought.

Didn't have to call that Bart.

Bart, he would have made fun of me.

♣ CHAPTER 25 ♣

I'm worried about you, Gabriel," said Bart. They were sitting at the bar in Toussaint. Susan Klein was in the cooler, making up an order. There was no one else in the place. The day outside was beautiful. The old drunks had come and gone, with their morning skinful, and the lunch crowd had yet to arrive.

"Unh?" said Du Pré. He was looking in the mirror, at the smoky and rippled images of the moldering big-game heads on the walls and the neon bleeding in the beer signs.

"You get this look," said Bart. "You can't just kill these people. Harvey's worried. He tells me he'll have to bust you, and since you were warned, he won't be feeling any too bad about it."

"Yah," said Du Pré. "Well, I am not worried."

Bart looked away. He shook his head.

"Interesting requests," he said. He was looking at a short piece of white paper, words in Du Pré's meticulous penmanship.

"Them FBI can't do this anyway," said Du Pré. "Me, I would just like to know where they go, maybe, I find a car I like to know that about."

"OK," said Bart. "I'll have them FedExed here."

Du Pré peeled five hundred dollars off the roll he carried and he handed it to Bart.

Bart started to open his mouth and then he took it.

"Good thing that you do for little Lourdes," said Du Pré.

Bart shrugged.

"I have money, Du Pré," he said. "I don't have a lot of wisdom."

Lourdes was spending the rest of the summer with a maiden aunt of Bart's, in Chicago. She was taking some classes at the Art Institute.

"Well," Bart had said to Lourdes, "I think you'd like to see a big city. Chicago's a big city. It ain't Seattle, but it'll have to do."

Lourdes had cried, packed a little bag, and flown out the next day.

"She want' to do *art*?" said Madelaine. "How come she don't say so to me?"

"You're her mother," said Bart.

"OK," said Madelaine. "Maybe you try it for a while."

"Poor Lourdes," said Bart. "Aunt Marella is very old-country."

"That mean that Lourdes is very safe," said Madelaine. "Me, I like that."

Du Pré cleared his throat.

"Um," said Du Pré. "How old are you, you have your first . . ."

"I am fifteen," said Madelaine.

"OK," said Du Pré. "I shut up now."

"Very smart man," said Madelaine.

"Harvey'll be here the day after tomorrow," said Bart. "He said he did want to come but he couldn't really justify it since he is just supervising Pidgeon. So I sent a plane for him."

"Unh," said Du Pré. "We go to the bar now."

Madelaine was building up a good head of steam. She would sometime in the next hour make Du Pré pay dearly for his impertinence, if Du Pré was stupid enough to wait for the explosion.

I wonder she is OK now, thought Du Pré. He diddled his drink. It was watery and the ice was about gone, but then, it was early in the day.

"I think I go on out to Benetsee's," said Du Pré. "That old man, he got to come back sometime."

"Oh," said Bart, "I don't know, he could just stay away and send you notes by coyote."

119

Du Pré laughed. He finished his drink and he got up and he went out to his old cruiser and he got in and started it and drove slowly out toward Benetsee's cabin.

He turned up the rutted, grassed-over drive and he thumped along over some sticks of firewood fallen off the truck that brought the last load in. The weeds thinned out when he got to the cabin. A half dozen fat Merino sheep guarded by a small sheepdog were cropping the growth.

Du Pré parked and he got out and he walked around the ramshackle cabin to the backyard where the sweat lodge stood. The doorflap was up and the fires cold.

Young-Man-Who-Has-No-Name was standing by the little brook, arms wrapped around, hands on his shoulders. He was praying. Du Pré sat on a big round of ponderosa that was a splitting block for the firewood, and he waited until the young man moved.

"You got a name yet?" said Du Pré.

The young man shook his head and he smiled.

"I don't miss it," he said. "You can be named for what is not there as well as for what is."

Du Pré walked over to where the young man stood. He looked at the brook. It was boiling with little trout. The fish were clotted together and dashing around a tiny pool.

A kingfisher's blue feather floated in the air.

OK, Du Pré thought, I don't even want to know.

"You hear from that Benetsee?" said Du Pré.

The young man nodded.

"He be back in the fall," he said. "Early fall maybe. Anyway he come he say before the first snow."

First fucking snow here maybe tomorrow, thought Du Pré, I been snowed on Fourth of July, end of July, first part of August. I been stuck up in the Wolfs a week once. Blizzard on the twentieth of August. First snow. Why he don't say when the sun shines sometimes?

"Your Madelaine send me some good food," said the young man. "She is a ver' good woman."

Du Pré nodded. Madelaine, she feed all the earth, wipe all of its tears, she could. But she fix about half of this county one way and another.

"Good you are here," said the young man. "That Jacqueline, she say I come to supper, maybe you come, too?"

Du Pré nodded. His daughter Jacqueline and her Raymond and their . . . fourteen children. Well, anyway the doctor say, no more, damn it. I tied your tubes. Next set of twins, you die, for sure.

Madelaine had talked with Jacqueline a long time when Jacqueline was in the hospital, last pair of babies almost kill her. At last, she nod and cry.

My son-in-law Raymond, he is looking very relieved these days. Feed all them kids, not too bad. Remember all the names of the kids these kids have, that is pret' bad. Me, I can't remember but about half my grandchildren. Names.

I only have the two before my wife, she dies.

Du Pré felt a tight feeling in this throat. He remembered his wife dying, her eyes burning bright, her dark hair sweaty, on the pillow.

Two little girls, my Jacqueline, my Maria, standing with me, I got hold of each little hand.

My wife she smile at us and she sigh long time and she is gone.

My girls they turn out pret' good. They take good care of me.

"I want to talk, that old bastard," said Du Pré, suddenly angry.

The young man stood smiling. He had very deep, gentle eyes. The world amused him, or he pitied it.

"Well," said Du Pré, "I don't guess I go and find him."

"Benetsee," laughed the young man, "he don't want to be found, he does not be found. Try to catch a coyote, a bucket?"

Du Pré laughed.

"He say to tell you that he thinks of you," said the young man. "How stupid you are. He wishes he could help that, but there is no cure."

Du Pré nodded.

"Tell him," said Du Pré, "I say, listen, old bastard, you go fuck a lame three-legged coyote, got clap."

The young man laughed. It was a laugh that rippled like water. A deep merriment.

"How you meet him?" said Du Pré.

The young man looked off at a magpie flying past.

"I am working, Calgary, and he . . . he come . . . tell me, quit what you are doing, wrong blood for it, so I do, and I am here."

"What work you doing?" said Du Pré.

The young man pursed his lips. He looked pained.

"Teaching," he said.

"OK," said Du Pré. "What you teaching?"

"Computers," said the young man.

"Christ," said Du Pré. "I thought you were a fucking longhair."

"Oh," said the young man. "Well, no, not then."

"He stick his head out of your computer?"

The young man shook his head.

"Christ," said Du Pré.

"Me," said the young man, "I don't talk about that. It was pretty scary, how it happened."

Du Pré heard a car come up the drive. It parked. The door chunked.

"Du Pré!" said Bart.

Du Pré turned.

"You'd better come."

"I need that damn Benetsee . . ." Du Pré said. He looked angrily at the young man.

"He say you don't," said the young man.

"God damn him," said Du Pré.

"Du Pré!" said Bart. He looked anguished, drained.

Du Pré walked to Bart.

"Where?" he said.

"Up on the Hi-Line," said Bart. "They just found her. It's out of the county, but you'd better go."

Du Pré felt a knot in his gut.

"It's the oldest Morissette girl," said Bart. "Her mother thought the kid had run away to Billings. She did it several times before."

Little Barbara Morissette.

Madelaine's niece.

The family lived in Toussaint.

Three houses from Madelaine.

✤ CHAPTER 26 ✤

D amned bad," said Sheriff Paton. "I been on this job thirty year and I never . . . animal did this dies. He dies. That's all."

There were three of Paton's deputies there. They all looked like they wanted very much to kill someone.

Little Barbara Morissette was lying on her back, naked, her legs spread, a tree branch shoved up her crotch.

And then her killer had sawed off her head and stuck it in a slash in her belly.

Nightmare.

Du Pré felt his eyes burn. He remembered the little auburn-haired girl. A sweet child. Musical.

Dead young woman.

Fifteen? Sixteen?

Madelaine will be praying.

Me, I am sick and mad.

Jesus.

Du Pré looked around the rest stop behind him. The girl was off in the brush behind the parking lot. She'd been there a little while. Not very long. Maybe left there last night.

Du Pré looked at the ground. No drag marks.

The Morissette girl was slender, small. A strong man could carry her easily.

Over his shoulder.

Cut her here.

The ground was black with old blood.

Green and blue bottleflies buzzed lazily around, laying eggs.

The cross, the notch, the place where they meet, Du Pré thought. On the Hi-Line.

They know about each other.

They have to.

Are they proud? Jealous? They get angry? When they get angry, does it make them stupid?

It makes me stupid.

I got to breathe right.

Think.

Damn Benetsee, I need his dreams.

Have to make do with my own. I quit whining now.

"Damn," said Sheriff Paton. "I ain't gonna sleep a while, here."

Du Pré looked at him. Tall man, thin, weathered to wrinkles and washed-out blue eyes behind bifocals. Wore a big hogleg. Probably a .44 Magnum. Light load. Probably killed a few in his time. Kind of Sheriff calls the crook, who he knows, and says, yeah, well, either you come on in or I come and get you. And that ain't gonna make my mood any too good.

They come right in, you bet.

The FBI arrived. Several vans filled with technicians and equipment.

One car which had Pidgeon in it and two men.

Pidgeon waved at Du Pré. She stuck her hands in the pocket of her light jacket and she came over. She stared for a long time at poor little Barbara Morissette.

She bent over to look closer.

She was biting her lower lip with her straight white teeth.

The crew of technicians assembled. They talked in hushed voices. Cameras. Measuring tapes. Black attaché cases. The technicians put on light blue coveralls.

Pidgeon came over to Du Pré and Sheriff Paton.

"Special Agent Pidgeon, FBI," said Pidgeon. She stuck out her hand. Paton took it and grasped it firmly. He looked into her eyes and he nodded.

"Yes, ma'am," he said.

Pidgeon smiled.

"When was she found?" she said.

" 'Fore daylight," said Paton. "Couple of . . . tourists was headed back here with a sleeping bag to, uh, take a nap. Stumbled over her."

Oh, thought Du Pré, there is one sex life shot for a while.

Pidgeon nodded.

"You know about this guy?" she said.

"Yup," said Paton. "We've had, oh, six, I guess, twenty year. Don't know if they was all his. Bastard."

"We'll find him," said Pidgeon.

"I expect you will," said Paton. "Now, you need anything you call Myra—she's the dispatcher—and I told her to arrange it. Myra lets me run for election and get shot at once in a while, but she runs the department. Always has."

"I'm the coroner, too," said Sheriff Paton. "I done all I have to. Pronounced her dead. Filled out a form. Some job. You find this s.o.b."

"We will," said Pidgeon.

"Um," said Sheriff Paton. "I'd best go. Got a wreck to sort out up the road."

"We passed it," said Pidgeon, "It looked pretty bad."

"Eighteen-wheeler hits a passenger car it's always pretty bad," said Paton. "Only this one flipped and killed the truck driver, too. Don't usually do that. I expect we'll find he was on pocket rockets. Long road. They gobble them speed pills, try to do fourteen–fifteen hundred miles in a straight twenty-four hours."

"Yeah," said Pidgeon.

"Can't blame 'em," said Paton. "Tryin' to make a livin'. It's not easy. I got a boy does that. Hope I don't have to scrape him off the side of this damn highway."

A couple big diesel trucks roared past.

The Sheriff walked away slowly. Loose. A little sad.

"She is my Madelaine's niece," said Du Pré. "My Madelaine, this girl's mother don't like each other much. But she will go crazy, it is someone her family, anyway."

"At least someone cares about her," said Pidgeon. "Most of 'em, no one gives a damn. But I was in Seattle, and I talked to a couple prostitutes who were scared, of course, and grieving for their friends. I hate this."

"How is that Harvey?" said Du Pré.

"Pain in the ass. Worried about you. He's gonna chew on you a lot when he sees you. He'd about just as soon kill these assholes with a shovel himself. You know, we're pretty good. We nail most bad guys, take a little time. But the serial killers are very hard to catch. And of serial killers, of course, the really intelligent ones are the worst and the hardest to catch. That little fuck Bundy wasn't all that smart, but he did some real damage. Green River Killer, not a trace. The Chain Killer, not a trace. There's a guy down South, burns his victims in the swamps. Does it when the swamps are burning. Not a trace."

"These guys leave some traces," said Du Pré.

"Yeah," said Pidgeon. "We just don't know which traces are theirs. This could take years, Du Pré."

Du Pré shook his head.

"Be over before the snow flies," he said.

Pidgeon looked at him.

"Well," said Pidgeon, "I guess I'll go watch the wizards there for a while, see what they find."

Du Pré looked down at his feet. There was a little scrap of clear plastic, the kind that packages some small object. He bent down and picked it up. Pretty heavy plastic.

"What you got there?" said Pidgeon.

"Piece of plastic," said Du Pré.

"All kinds of crap blows over here from the highway and the rest stop," said Pidgeon. "I want it though. We'll see how long it's been in the sun, at least."

They walked over to where the technicians were working. Two of them were zipping up a heavy yellow body bag. They rolled the filled bag onto a stretcher and carried it off to a morgue wagon.

A couple of blue-suited men were minutely examining the ground that the body had lain on.

They kept their faces close, but didn't put their hands down on the bloody earth.

One of the two slipped a dentist's pick from his pocket and he prised something up out of the dirt. He lifted it and dropped it in a little plastic bag, already numbered. He straightened up and made some notes.

"This one is the Hi-Line Killer," said Du Pré.

"Um," said Pidgeon.

Or maybe not, Du Pré thought. Maybe it is Come-to-Jesus, trying to look like the Hi-Line Killer.

Maybe they tease each other with dead young women. See, I got her before you did.

I got to think like them sometime and I don't want to.

Got to find out what their dreams are.

Be in those dreams.

Maybe I get close and make them run.

Hunt them like the coyote hunts. One coyote, chase until he is tired, run that rabbit in a circle, then the other one take over, and so on, till that rabbit is run to death.

Something like that.

Young-Man-Who-Has-No-Name. Old Benetsee, he is some coyote himself.

Always joking.

Tells coyote stories.

God's dogs. They must know everything. Me, I always told everything to my dog and I don't hardly know nothing.

"Du Pré," said Pidgeon, "you please give my love to Madelaine."

"You be down?" said Du Pré.

"No," said Pidgeon, "I'm going with little Barbara, talk to her when they do the autopsy. I do that when I can."

"What do you say?" said Du Pré. "When you are there?"

"I'll say, Barbara, I'm so sorry. I need your help now. I promise you I will find this man. And he won't do this to anyone else after I do."

"Good," said Du Pré. "I tell my Madelaine that."

✦ CHAPTER 27 ✦

I don't know how he gets that damn plane down on that rotten little piece of runway you think is an airport," said Harvey. "Christ, my asshole was in my throat. I ate my worry beads. I thought of my orphaned children and beautiful, impoverished widow. I thought of the asshole who would follow after me with my beautiful, impoverished widow. I hated him. Christ."

Du Pré laughed. Harvey had always hated flying. He was a worrier.

The little jet had screamed in and the pilot had set it down and reversed the thrust of the engines. Du Pré well remembered being thrown against the seat belt. Sometimes there were cows, sheep, and horses in the field at the end of the runway. Sometimes they were on the runway since the rancher who owned the pasture at the end of it was careless about the fencing.

Small jet hit a cow, that is all, Du Pré thought. It would fold up pretty good.

Harvey Wallace, tall and thin and lean and dark and sardonic. Also Harvey Weasel Fat, a Blackfeet boy made good.

Mean bastards them Blackfeet, Du Pré thought, sit out there on the prairie without any cover. Have to be mean. Remember them Athapascans, Du Pré thought, some of them old songs, they describe the Athapascans come down that Great North Trail. They come from the north slope of the Himalayas. They are mean bastards. Them

128

slaves, them Apaches, them Navajos, them Haida. Cannibals and fighters.

Come down the Great North Trail, from Asia over them Bering Straits, down the inside of the Rockies. Not so long ago. Them Haida trade with Japan and China. They leave them Queen Charlotte Islands, go across the North Pacific, some woman singer with a song tells them how to get there sings that song. Get home, sing the song backwards.

Mean bastards. Run us Cree the hell east. Run the Sioux south and east. We get guns from the whites and come back.

Things were not so peaceful then.

"Du Pré," said Harvey, "what you been thinkin'?"

Du Pré started. He had forgotten that Harvey was there. Standing next to his bag.

"I am sorry," said Du Pré. He picked up Harvey's bag.

They walked to Du Pré's old cruiser.

The little jet had turned around and the pilot had jammed the little plane down the runway and into the air and the roaring shriek was fading.

"How is Madelaine?" said Harvey.

"Not so good," said Du Pré. "Her cousin's girl, you know. Madelaine, she is helping her cousin, the sorrow. We are having a wake."

Harvey nodded.

"Songs, some old dances, the brothers and sisters of Barbara they are very sad. Mother is sad. Madelaine don't much like her cousin— never mention her name, I know her only as Mrs. Morissette. Morissette, him killed working on railroad, eight, ten years ago."

Harvey nodded.

"Madelaine probably dance with you, though," said Du Pré.

"Dance with a Blackfeet," said Harvey.

"My Madelaine, she is very liberal woman," said Du Pré. "I think she even dance with a Mormon."

"That's pretty liberal," said Harvey. "OK, what'd Pidgeon think?"

Du Pré shrugged. He didn't know what Pidgeon thought.

"It is either that Hi-Line guy or the other one or someone trying to make us think it is him," said Du Pré. "How anyone know anything?"

Harvey nodded.

They walked to Du Pré's old cruiser. Grasshoppers whirred past. A few of the dusty locusts, black wings with yellow borders.

Du Pré stuck Harvey's bag in the backseat.

They got in.

Du Pré started the car and he turned it around and headed for Toussaint. They were at the little airfield in Cooper. Bart had paid to have the runway lengthened so small private jets could land.

Du Pré rolled a cigarette. He lit it.

Harvey picked up the little cardboard box on the seat.

"Very nice," he said. "When you get these?"

"Couple days," said Du Pré.

"Well," said Harvey, "you stick the beeper on a car and this receiver will tell you right where the car is, up to fifty miles. Tell you if it is moving, where, and if it's headed to you how long it will be before it gets there."

"Always wanted one," said Du Pré.

Twelve big grain trucks passed them heading toward the elevators in Cooper. There was a railroad spur there, and huge towering metal silos to hold the grain. Some ranchers were selling the wheat right from the fields, some were storing it and hoping that the price would rise and not fall.

Du Pré parked in front of the Toussaint bar. There were a lot of cars, mostly old and shabby, parked around.

"The wake is here?" said Harvey.

"Yah," said Du Pré. "Can't have booze at the schools and so it is here. We don't got too many buildings, rent."

Toussaint had maybe fifty houses and those were mostly trailers. Poor little town. Lots of Métis. Poor people.

There were a few more expensive houses, not many.

Harvey and Du Pré got out. They went on in.

The place was packed.

Over in one corner Mrs. Morissette was sitting, receiving people who were bearing condolences. There was a trestle table filled with casseroles and salads and Susan had a huge joint of beef set under a heat lamp on a serving table. A rancher stood near it, ready to slice off the meat.

"You hungry?" said Du Pré.

"Starved," said Harvey. "I can't eat before I fly. After, I am ravenous. I escaped the fiery splat once more."

Susan poured Du Pré a drink. She looked at Harvey.

"Hmmmm," he said. "Bloody Mary?"

Susan nodded. Du Pré tilted his head toward the book she kept tabs in. She would write the drinks down.

Damn, Du Pré thought, I must pay my tab, can't remember when I did that last.

Harvey went off to get a plate of food.

"Susan," said Du Pré, "I pay my tab?"

"You got money on it," said Susan.

"Damn Bart?" said Du Pré.

"Lips are sealed, Gabriel," said Susan. "I think you still got a thousand in credit."

Bart, sure enough.

"Look," said Susan, "Bart's frustrated. He wants to do something about all this horror. He just came in and slapped the money down and he cleared off all the tabs. People he doesn't even know."

"Well," said Du Pré, "I guess he don't know all the people make the money for him, either."

Susan laughed.

"Benny's coming along pretty quick," she said. "Had a fight out on one of the ranches, some pair of kids with a combine crew got into it. One kid hit the other with a wrench."

Du Pré nodded.

"One got hit had to be taken to the hospital, then flown down to Billings. Head injury. Don't know how bad, but it must be pretty bad. Anyway, Benny had to arrest the other one and book him."

So he can sit on his ass, jail, wonder if it is manslaughter or just assault he is guilty of. Everybody wonder that until the guy in the hospital either makes it or he does not.

Mrs. Morissette began to shriek. Several women went to her and they held her. She wailed.

That bitch don't even really mean it, Du Pré thought.

Madelaine looked over at Du Pré, then up to the ceiling.

OK, thought Du Pré, I am right, once.

Harvey was sitting at a table far away from the knot around Mrs. Morissette. He was eating like he hadn't for days.

Him probably not eat for days. Pretty brave guy, fly when it do that to him, Du Pré thought, me, I just have the shits bad for three days before I got to fly. It don't bother me.

I don't like this twentieth century. Won't like that twenty-first one, either. I am sure of it.

Madelaine left the little group and she came over and she put her arms around Du Pré and she kissed him.

"You bring back that ugly Blackfeet," said Madelaine.

"Had to," said Du Pré. "I was the only car there."

"You think his dick is as big as I hear?" said Madelaine.

Du Pré shrugged.

"OK," said Madelaine. "I just wondered."

Du Pré shrugged.

"Maybe I dance with him," she went on.

Du Pré smelled the wine on Madelaine's breath.

She is some upset, he thought.

She is angry, me, because she is angry about poor little Barbara Morissette.

That son of a bitch doing this, he is spoiling a lot.

Du Pré sipped his drink.

✤ CHAPTER 28 ✤

Booger Tom squinted at the hot noon sun riding high across the sky. The sky was white with dust and heat. The light was tight and tough. It bleached out all the colors and the clouds of chaff blowing off the big combines glinted like flakes of metal in the air.

"One hot bastard," said Booger Tom.

Du Pré nodded. He had spent a lot of time harvesting and he didn't remember it fondly. The Saturdays in the bars after he had been paid off were fun, other than the two times he had been arrested along with the rest of the crew.

Some of them tough little Montana towns did that. Peel your summer wages in fines for disorderly conduct and run you out of the county.

Summer wages.

"I never did this," said Harvey. "I was always brown-nosing so I could go to summer school. I hate the outdoors. It's dirty. Bugs fuck in it. Not a good address."

Booger Tom looked at Harvey and he grinned.

"Got to get you up on a horse," he said.

"A horse?" said Harvey, eyes wide in horror.

"Yeah," said Booger Tom. "Like the ones you done rode in the rodeo. Quit pissin' on my boots, callin' it a rainstorm. I know who you are."

"Who is he?" said Du Pré.

"He rodeoed some," said Booger Tom. "Pretty good, too."

"I hated it," said Harvey.

Du Pré laughed.

"Well," said Harvey, "I needed a scholarship so I could go to college and rodeo . . ."

"Got ya laid more often than football," said Booger Tom. "I known you bastards all of my life."

The big combines were rolling on, blades slowly pushing the stalks of grain into the cutters.

Then one of them jerked abruptly.

They could hear a deep whannnnggggg over the roar of the engines.

The combine stopped.

Steam shot out of the engine.

"Shit," said Booger Tom. He was looking off toward the west. The sky was clear. "It's gonna rain round midnight. Shit. Got to get that damn grain in."

Someone from the combine crew was loping over the huge field to a pickup truck. They climbed in the cab and picked up the radio mike and talked.

"Damn downtime costs one-fifty an hour," said Booger Tom.

"Lawyers cost more than that," said Harvey.

Booger Tom snorted.

"So what are we doing today?" said Harvey. "I get to meet that guy who's out at Benetsee's?"

"Sure," said Du Pré. "We maybe get some lunch and then we can go, sure."

He led Harvey and Booger Tom into Bart's house.

The refrigerator was chock full of smoked salmon, pâté, caviar, and salad stuff. Some good wines, white ones, chilled. Bart didn't drink but he knew what went with what.

"My my," said Harvey. "Two months of my pitiful salary is sitting in that refrigerator. Those are two-kilogram tins of Beluga. Cherkassy. I never even heard of Cherkassy. The salmon comes from England, I bet."

"Iceland," said Du Pré.

"Oh," said Harvey, "great. Any capers?"

Du Pré sighed and he opened a cupboard and took out a tall narrow bottle.

"The guys at the office will never believe this," said Harvey. "I think I saw an open bottle of Graves in there."

Du Pré fished it out.

"I think I'll have a baloney sandwich," said Booger Tom.

"I get a hamburger later," said Du Pré.

"Barbarians," said Harvey, dipping a water biscuit into the caviar.

"Fish slime," said Booger Tom.

"The two of you can fuck off and go outside you don't like it," said Harvey, "but I will eat like a hog in peace. Or death."

"C'mon, Du Pré," said Booger Tom. "I got some ham and . . . you know, food over to my place."

They went out the back door and toward Booger Tom's little cabin. It was the oldest building on the ranch, perhaps a century old.

Tom opened the sagging door and he and Du Pré went in to a boar's nest. Saddles on trees, horsehair ropes and hackamores, racks of guns, and the stink of old unwashed socks.

"Awful, ain't it?" said Tom. He led Du Pré back outside and to a small brown clapboard building twenty feet away.

A little cookhouse.

It was spotless. A pump by the sink, a big old Clarion woodstove. A stainless steel monitor top refrigerator.

Tom brought out ham and mustard and he took bread out of a breadsafe and plates—battered blue enameled tin ones—out of the standing cupboard.

They ate in the shade behind the cookhouse, under the hanging runners of a weeping willow. A little creek purled by the picnic table.

"Fish eggs," said Booger Tom. "And Frog piss."

Du Pré laughed. So much for Bart's two-hundred-dollar-a-bottle wine. Frog piss.

"He's all right, that Harvey," said Tom. "I remember him from Rapid City, maybe. Took a dive into a chute to try to save a rider who'd gone under a Brahma. Saved the guy, too. Broke Harvey's arm, though, put him out of the money."

Du Pré nodded.

Tom dug four beers out of the creek and they each had two of them.

"Beer's a better kind of cold out of a crick," said Tom.

They ate and drank and smoked.

The day stayed hot.

They ambled back to Bart's.

Du Pré looked out in the field. The combine had a couple men on it, and there was another man in mechanic's coveralls leaned into the engine compartment. He reached a hand back and another man handed him a tool.

Du Pré looked at the dark green van.

The guy who saved my ass, up north, there. Simpson.

Everything was dusty. The van was spotless. The dark windows gleamed.

Du Pré rolled a cigarette.

"You be careful with that," said Booger Tom.

Du Pré nodded. He smoked the cigarette and then he crushed it with his bootheel.

"Think I'll walk out there, see what they are doing," he said.

"Too damn hot," said Booger Tom. "I'll let you."

"Tell Harvey I be right back," said Du Pré.

Du Pré climbed through the fence across the road and he walked through the chaff and broken stalks toward the down combine. The other one had kept going. Two idle trucks sat at the edge of the field. The drivers were sleeping in the shade.

Du Pré's boots crackled on the dry stalks. The stalks were slippery. He had to lean a little forward and walk on the balls of his feet to keep his balance.

A magpie flew past, low.

Only damn bird I ever saw tail was longer than it is, maybe a peacock, thought Du Pré.

Simpson pulled his head out of the engine compartment of the combine. He pulled a red rag from his coveralls and he wiped the sweat from his forehead. He said something to the man who had handed him the tool and the man went back to the van and he opened the rear doors and he climbed inside. He was in there for only a moment and then he got out carrying a red metal case and a paper sack.

Simpson took the case and he opened it and selected a socket and he took something out of the paper sack and he leaned back in the engine compartment.

He stayed hunched over for ten minutes.

Du Pré could see him straining as he heaved on the wrench.

He came out and wiped his forehead again.

Du Pré was standing very near.

He watched as Simpson made some minor adjustments.

Simpson signaled the driver to try it.

The starter ground and the engine caught and the exhaust stack belched black smoke.

The driver revved the engine.

Simpson reached back in the engine compartment and then he stood back and nodded and he closed the cover. Flipped the latches on.

The driver gave him a thumbs-up.

Simpson and his assistant took the tools back to the van. Simpson got in and he waited for the assistant to hand him tools. He stowed them.

The assistant walked away.

Simpson got out. He saw Du Pré and he waved and smiled.

He went round to the driver's door of the van and he got in and he drove off.

Du Pré watched him go.

Du Pré walked slowly back to Bart's house. The trip back seemed a lot shorter.

Harvey was sitting on the porch, drinking a glass of white wine.

"What's up?" he said to Du Pré.

Du Pré shrugged.

♣ CHAPTER 29 ♣

We did that," said Harvey. "We hired psychics. What we may or may not have found out I couldn't really tell you. Sometimes we'd think that they'd been helpful, but, then, we'd run probability studies and it could as easily have been chance. You know, the old cop method. You spread enough glue around and your fly will step in it. You look at enough evidence, ten thousand things, and you find one thing that starts a chain of deductions. My math isn't good. We hired mathematicians. The Bureau doesn't like to talk about it. Truth is, though, that serial killers are the same and not the same, and that they are largely fairly stupid and survive a while because they are unpredictable. The ones worry me are the smart ones. About as many, proportionately, as there are very smart people. Not many. Not many. And it's hard enough to catch the dumb ones. Maybe we never caught a smart one. Maybe we just never did."

"Yah," said Du Pré. "Well, how 'bout astrologers?"

"Oh, yes," said Harvey.

"I am kidding," said Du Pré.

"I'm not," said Harvey. "We did. I remember one woman . . . I liked her. She was very humble and sweet and smart. She said it was a mistake to think that astrology delivered truth as it was a mistake to think that the Bible does. The truths in both were poetic. They were both ways of looking at the world that was not rational. That astrology was a means of interpreting lives and fates. But that to try to jam it into a box was foolish. She said in her world, the serial killers and certain other people—we call them sociopaths—were called "elementals." They were all by themselves. They were unable to grasp that there was anything in all the world but them. That the world existed to please them. And that they could charm but never love. They are all pretty charming. I thought she was nuts, until I remembered that I never had one of these assholes in hand but that they tried to charm me. Tried to explain away what had happened. Even to convince me that what had happened actually didn't. *And for them it didn't happen.*"

"Shit," said Du Pré. "Your damn elementals just sound like most teenage kids."

"That's a bit harsh," said Harvey.

Du Pré shrugged.

Harvey looked away.

"All right," he said. "Teenage kids are like that, but only some of the time. They learn. They grow up. Sociopaths don't."

"You know," said Du Pré, "trouble with words like that is that if you can pronounce them you think you know what they mean. And if you think that you know what they mean, you think that you know something."

"Jesus," said Harvey. "You studying philosophy these days?"

"No," said Du Pré. "I am just talking bullshit."

They were sitting at a picnic table at Raster Creek, waiting on Rolly Challis.

"Here I am, a good FBI man, talking bullshit with a loose cannon who I will probably have to arrest later on waiting on a bank robber I couldn't catch," said Harvey, grinning. "The smile is just for jollies."

"Harvey," said Du Pré, "how many these dead women we talking about? Eh? Lot of them. Me, I just am going to make it stop. I don't embarrass you. You worry too much."

"I don't worry too much," said Harvey. "I know you two fuckers."

"What I do make you feel like this?" said Du Pré. "I only shoot that asshole shooting at me. Remember? I shoot me, too."

"Oh," said Harvey. "The brand inspection that went wrong."

"Yeah," said Du Pré. "I shoot me in the belly while I am being such a badass gunfighter. Then I shoot at guy who is shooting at me and I am lucky and he is not. I shoot him right through the heart. I don't even look at him, Harvey, I am just hoping to spoil his aim or something."

"I wasn't thinking about that," said Harvey.

"Lucky, he fall and break his neck," said Du Pré. "I am not there."

"Whatever," said Harvey wearily.

"OK," said Du Pré. "This Simpson he fit that list that Pidgeon sent."

"Sure," said Harvey. "So does any other compulsive guy keeps his rig neat and does a good job and who is a very loud Christian."

"But we don't know the times so good," said Du Pré.

"Bodies lie out there months or years, no shit," said Harvey.

"Hi-Line Killer," said Du Pré, "he travels this Highway 2."

"He's got to be a truck driver," said Harvey.

"Maybe a salesman," said Du Pré.

"Big route," said Harvey. "It's two thousand miles one way."

"I think that is Rolly," said Du Pré. A big truck was coming up the far side of the hill to the west.

The square black cab lifted into view.

Rolly.

Du Pré and Harvey sat silent. The big truck was moving fast. Then Rolly began to slow it down. He choked back his speed and rolled into the parking area and stopped. The air brakes hissed and set and the big diesel popped at lowest idle.

Rolly sat in the cab for a couple minutes. When he dropped like a gymnast to the ground he had on his big black hat. He grinned at Du Pré and Harvey, and sauntered up.

"Mornin', Du Pré," he said, eyes twinkling, "and Agent Wallace."

"Rolly," said Harvey, "don't be a prick. I have a headache."

"I got aspirin in the truck," said Rolly.

"No," said Harvey. "It's bad for my stomach."

Rolly grinned and he shook with silent laughter.

"You got something," he said suddenly.

"We always hope that we do," said Harvey.

Rolly nodded. He moved his chew of snoose a little in his cheek.

"I been thinking wrong all this time," said Rolly. "You know. I

140

thought it had to be a truck driver on the Hi-Line, here. But now I don't think so."

Harvey looked at him.

"The places where the bodies were dumped," said Rolly. "A truck would be too conspicuous. Have to leave it by the side of the road. It would be reported. Too obvious. Nope, it's got to be someone else. Could be a salesman, or even some guy just likes to drive back and forth."

"We checked all that," said Harvey. "Looked for radiuses. There aren't all that many places on the Hi-Line to gas up. Asked if there was anyone who fit that. Just a driver, always coming through. Course, we got a lot of names and leads, but they were all salesmen. Checked out all of the salesmen and none of their routes and times fit all the bodies. This guy at least pretty well displays his victims. We find some of them the morning after. No names came up in the soup."

"You've been *working?*" said Rolly.

"Fuck you, Challis," said Harvey. "I am ready for any suggestions."

"Guy's thought of about everything," said Rolly. "He'd think of showing up at gas stations too often. Cafés. He'd be real careful."

"No shit," said Harvey.

"You got a profile?" said Rolly.

"Pidgeon's sure the guy's pissed. Abused child. He displays his victims. He may well have a juvenile record, but probably nothing else."

"What I hear," said Rolly, "is that the guy strangles. Often uses drugs. Lorazepam and alcohol. Big doses. Big deal. You can get benzodiazipines on the street like you can get peanuts in a ballpark. Booze is easy."

Harvey nodded.

"Pinch is the gas," said Rolly.

Harvey nodded.

"Guy's got a van," said Harvey, "and that van has a couple fifty-five-gallon drums in the rear. Plus the tank."

Harvey looked at him.

"Fifteen hundred miles," he said.

"He'll get it filled," said Rolly. "Has to. Oh, he can get a tank easy enough, that's four hundred or so. But where does he go for a big fill? Got to be a farm. Got some cover anyway."

"We thought of it," said Harvey, "but thought it was too far-fetched. I think what we thought of it was we couldn't figure out how to find a hundred-gallon fill, one hundred thirty, when the guy didn't want us to find it."

"Or five, six fills in a big city, those gasamat places, move around. Kids in the booths are minimum wage and they don't stay long."

"And he wouldn't fuck with the license plates," said Harvey.

"Have to buy a lot of tires," said Rolly.

"Yeah," said Harvey. "Every fifty thousand miles he would. That's a dozen full circles. He probably doesn't do that many full circles."

"More bodies the closer you get to Yakima," said Rolly. "He favors the lee side of the Cascades."

"We're getting pretty specific," said Harvey.

"Yeah," said Rolly. "But what else works?"

Du Pré rolled a smoke. He looked off toward the south. The Wolf Mountains were down there, but the earth's curve covered them.

I got that Simpson, Du Pré thought, it is him. But this guy, I got to hunt him. How do you hunt, the old way? You dream the deer and the deer come. You dream the buffalo and they come. You got to call them, then they come.

When we were trapping, did we dream the wolf? The marten? Them fisher cat? What they all do, that we dream them.

Du Pré rolled a cigarette.

Damn Benetsee.

I go to talk to Young-Man-Who-Has-No-Name.

Dream what it is that you hunt.

Du Pré lit his cigarette.

"I have one of those?" said Rolly.

Du Pré nodded.

✤ CHAPTER 30 ✤

Du Pré woke in the night. Madelaine was sleeping hard, her breath soft and steady. She had an arm flung out, hanging off the bed. She often slept like that.

Du Pré slipped out of bed and he wrapped a robe around his body and he padded out to the back porch. The air was thick and smelled of lightning. Then there was a great flash above and the rain lashed down. Huge drops thick together. Lightning flashed. Du Pré saw a cat dash across the grass and dive under the garden shed.

He was half-asleep. The images burned in his brain from the faded flashes and he thought he saw Benetsee faint, white-haired, in the misty shadows among the elms and willows by the little creek.

Du Pré went out the back door and he squelched across the grass in his bare feet. He was soaked halfway there. He stepped into the line of trees and stopped on the bank of the little spring creek.

The lightning flashed so close overhead he crouched.

He was chilled. He went back to the house and he took the sopping robe off and he hung it on the back porch and he walked softly naked to the bathroom and he toweled himself off and he went to the kitchen and he rolled a cigarette and he sat there smoking. He was wide-awake after his cold shower.

He sighed. He poured some whiskey in a tumbler and ran tap water in the whiskey until it was very pale and then he drank the ditch down all at once. It bloomed in his stomach, hot.

Good that they got all the wheat in tonight, Du Pré thought. Now the crews will go a little east, some maybe north to Alberta.

The weather had been fine.

It was four in the morning. The crews would have closed the bar in Toussaint.

The tracking beeper Harvey had brought him from Washington lay on the kitchen table. Du Pré dressed, pocketed the beeper, and he went out and walked down toward the bar. He stumbled once in a pothole. His cowboy boots were slick on the gumbo. He came through the trees in the little park across from the bar. The motor homes were all dark, compressors whirring.

Simpson's van was parked in the light from the spot on the front of the bar. Du Pré made his way round. He listened for dogs, but didn't hear any.

When he got to the van he peeled the sheet of plastic from the beeper, exposing the sticky base. It was modeled to look like a gob of mud. Du Pré reached high inside a back wheelwell and stuck the little electronic device to the clean metal.

Damn Simpson, he probably scrub this by hand with his bifocals on, Du Pré thought. Maybe not.

He backed away and went back to Madelaine's and he undressed and got into bed. He dozed for an hour and then he got up and made himself some breakfast and he ate and then he went out and got in his old cruiser. He switched on the tracking unit and a small green light came on. It showed Simpson's van within six hundred yards of Madelaine's, directly to the east. Du Pré nodded. The sun was rising that way.

OK.

Du Pré drove downtown and he parked beside the bar and he put the tracking unit on the transmission case and he lay down and he dozed.

The people in the motor homes came to life. Doors opened and shut. Engines caught. A couple of the motor homes lumbered out of the parking lot and went to the main street and then turned and headed out to the highway.

Simpson's van was still there in the campground across from the bar.

Du Pré waited.

For an hour.

Simpson finally came out of the motor home he shared with two other men. One of the men joked with him through the door. Simpson was carrying a cup of coffee, a road cup, one with a narrow top and a wide base.

He got in his van and he carefully warmed it up. He checked the windshield wipers. He leaned out and fiddled with the rearview mirror.

Then he drove briskly out and turned toward the highway.

Du Pré waited for a few minutes. Then he followed. If Simpson went west, he was headed north. If east, east. South, south, but Du Pré didn't think he would head that way.

Du Pré followed down to the intersection where Simpson would go either north or east. He went east.

There was no place to turn off that made any sense for the next hundred miles. Du Pré stayed twenty miles back. The green light was east of him. Simpson traveled at sixty-five miles an hour, exactly.

The liquid crystal display barely altered at all. Nothing out here. Once Simpson slowed down to thirty-five.

He find one cow on that road, thought Du Pré. About twenty miles he is either going to Miles City, or Plentywood.

Simpson took the road to Miles City. Du Pré followed five or six miles back. Simpson kept on at sixty-five.

Longest damn time I ever take, get to Miles City, Du Pré thought. Course I am not carrying a dead body I don't want found, so I am careless with the law.

Simpson stopped at the north edge of Miles City and he got gas. Du Pré waited by the road until Simpson moved again and then he drove on into town. Simpson was maybe a mile away, stopped. Du Pré got a tankful and he checked the oil and the belts on the engine and he shook his head when he spotted the hose that Simpson had stuck in his engine a few days before.

Me, I wonder he got an expensive set of black steel sockets, Du Pré thought.

Got maybe a folding rubber sheet in the back. Thick one. Blood-proof.

Got a box of small knives with leaf blades sunk in black plastic handles. Made in Taiwan.

Maybe got a box of earrings, rings, bracelets.

Crucifixes.

Maybe a map, got marks on it.

Take it out to jerk off to, those lonely nights.

I hope that I am right, Du Pré thought.

I don't like them Christer sons of bitches anyway, they spend their time howling about love and meaning death.

Du Pré pissed and he went back out to his cruiser and he drove on into Miles City and he had a good lunch at a saloon, a prime rib sandwich and some beer, a good salad he made up himself from the offerings on a big steel cart.

He rolled a smoke and had it and then another. Had another beer.

He paid and left and he drove toward the place that the green light said Simpson's van was parked at. It was in front of a church, a low cinder-block building. There was a big banner hanging from a side-wall which said "REVIVAL MEETING TONIGHT."

Du Pré drove out to the airport and he found a rental-car place had two little old sedans in the lot. There was no one in the office. A sign on the counter said, "If you want a car, call 788-9081." A telephone sat next to the sign.

A woman answered Du Pré's call.

"I need to rent a car," he said.

"Sure," she said. "I'll be right on down soon's as I get the kids out the door to school. Lunch. About half hour."

"OK," said Du Pré.

"If you want a beer there's some in a little icebox under the counter," she said. "Just lift up the passage gate and go on round."

"Thanks," said Du Pré.

He found the beer and he sat and waited outside in the shade, smoking and sipping beer. The woman came and she rented him a little brown Colt for twenty-five dollars.

"Just gas it up before you bring it back, please," she said, "or leave a few bucks if you don't have time. Leave the keys on the counter."

Du Pré nodded.

He went on into town in the little car. He stopped at a discount store and he bought a white straw hat and some big sunglasses and a loud silly shirt, one with huge tropical flowers on it in horrible colors.

I don't look like no Métis, Du Pré thought, driving back by the church. I am not buying those sandals. Maybe I go, though, to this revival meeting.

He went back to the discount store and he bought some cheap baggy cotton pants in a pale tan and some dirty-looking running shoes.

Full service, Du Pré thought, they get your shoes dirty, too.

He bought some tailor-made cigarettes. A butane lighter. His shepherd's lighter was unusual, length of rope and a striker.

I am some deep undercover, Du Pré thought. Feel like an asshole. Bitch bitch bitch.

There was a big tent at the back of the church. Du Pré parked a ways away and he went to the tent and looked in.

Simpson and three other men were sawing boards and nailing together a stage. They worked quickly and competently.

Du Pré nodded.

He went to a motel and he rented a room and he slept for five hours.

The green light on the tracking unit hadn't moved.

He went to the revival meeting at seven.

There were a hundred people there.

Simpson sat in the front row of folding chairs. He was well dressed, in a dark suit and shoes, a white shirt and a dark tie. His hair was pomaded.

The congregation sang loud hymns.

There was a choir. One of the singers was a pretty blond girl, blooming with what beauty she would have before going to fat and bad makeup in five years time.

147

Du Pré looked at Simpson.

Simpson stared at the girl.

He was wearing tinted glasses.

But his head never moved.

❧ CHAPTER 31 ❧

Du Pré sat in the sweat lodge. It was pitch-dark. The steam was so hot and close his lungs cleared of the tobacco he smoked. He coughed once. He inhaled deeply. The paint on his face clogged his pores. Sweat ran from his skin in streams.

He was alone. He dipped a little water from the bowl with a piece of curved birch bark and he sprinkled it on the red-hot stones. They glowed very dimly, and gave no light. They floated in his eyes. He could not really say where up and down were. He was sitting, but he felt so light he could have been sitting on the tight canvas of the ceiling.

Young-Man-Who-Has-No-Name sat outside. He was drumming. The strokes and rhythms multiplied.

No one man could do all that, Du Pré thought, I am a musician. He is drumming in straight time, nine-five time, thirteen-five time, backbeats. I have listened to drumming my whole life, I never heard this.

Young-Man-Who-Has-No-Name began to sing. The wailing ululations, prayers and offerings.

Du Pré's blood sang.

He bowed his head and he wept. His tears fell with his sweat.

I ask for many things. I ask for strength and cunning. I ask for courage. I ask for a warrior's heart. The heart of a warrior is his humility, the strength of the tribe is the warrior's humility. We are very small on this earth but we have our place.

Du Pré breathed.

He cleared his mind and he let the drumming and singing flow into his breath and blood.

He dreamed.

He woke slowly. His back was cold. He was lying on his back. He could feel the rough stems of grass against his skin. He looked up. The stars were out, a fingernail moon.

"Uh, Du Pré," said Benetsee.

Du Pré's eyes shot wide-open.

"You don't move or I don't talk to you," said Benetsee.

Du Pré froze.

That old shit, he thought, here he is. Play his damn games with me. Fucker.

"You doin' ver' good," said Benetsee.

Du Pré waited.

"You keep doin' that."

A wind came up. The willows sighed.

Du Pré waited.

He heard an owl call softly.

Felt wings brush his face.

Hush Wings. Owl's a good hunter. At night. Blind in the sun, the sport of starlings, then.

Du Pré heard the coyotes start to howl, the hunting chorus. The yips died away.

He sat up and he looked around.

Young-Man-Who-Has-No-Name was sitting with his legs tucked under him, head bowed. He held a bundle wrapped in marten skins.

Du Pré stood up. He went to the plank table he had piled his clothes on before he went into the sweat lodge. He toweled off and he dressed. His socks were damp and his boots were hard to get on. He rolled a smoke and he lit it and he looked up at the stars.

Far away, he thought, they don't need to bother with us. We can find our way around the world with them, though.

Du Pré glanced at Benetsee's praying apprentice.

Young-Man-Who-Has-No-Name hadn't moved.

Du Pré walked round the cabin to his cruiser and he reached in and got his whiskey and he had a little. He went back.

The young man was sitting on the table. He was smiling.

"OK," said Du Pré. "Where is that Benetsee?"

"I am in Canada, you fool," said the young man.

But it was Benetsee's old cracked voice.

Du Pré looked at him.

"Shit," he said.

He went to his car and got in and he drove. He didn't care where to. He drove west, out on dirt roads that wound through the rolling giant High Plains. He didn't know where he was going. He didn't care.

He came to a side road that cut across a hayfield set beneath a sheer scarp. Old pishkun. Buffalo Jump.

Du Pré took the road right up to the place where the boulders that had been spilled off the front lip were piled.

He got out and looked up at the rim.

There was just enough starlight to see faint dapples of lighter color. The grass that tongued up the watercourses.

Water and rock, water always wins in the end.

Du Pré stared hard.

He saw shadows, giant ones, tumbling through the air. The ghosts of buffalo bellowing as they fell. The hunters danced in triumph on the lip. The shaman lay broken on the rocks below. This was done once a generation, one time, use the pishkun. Plenty of meat. The shaman led them over the edge. He was singing.

The women butchered and dried meat and they danced.

The ground was black with blood.

The wolves and bears smelled the meat and they came.

Ravens, magpies, badgers, skunks, the vultures and the insects.

The eagles.

Up top there were some pits where eagle-catchers had lain hidden, a prairie chicken tethered close against the crisscrossed sticks above them. The eagle swooped and grasped the grouse in its talons and the eagle-catcher reached up and grabbed the eagle's legs and pulled down so that the eagle couldn't reach the hands with its beak.

It did not work that well, I bet, thought Du Pré.

Them shamans they are missing some fingers them eagles cut right off.

Shaman's bones right here, down in the rocks, under the grass.

Du Pré had hundreds of arrowheads and spearpoints and scrapers. He had been finding them since he was a child.

Gopher mounds were good places, new cuts where a stream was changing course, any place where a bulldozer churned the earth.

Du Pré sat and he smoked and he looked up at the scarp.

That is that kind of hunting. Me, I cannot stampede them Christers over a cliff. They do that for themselves.

What am I hunting?

A bad man.

What does he hunt.

Stupid young women.

Where does he go to feed.

To church.

Where does he go to drink?

No bars, they are sinful.

Where does he sleep?

Du Pré blew up. He got out of his car and he yelled and his voice boomed against the cliffs and rang back. Birds chirred, wakened. He kicked the door of his cruiser and he dented it. He grabbed his 9mm and he fired a whole clip at a boulder and the last round whanged off in a banshee scream, flattened to a disc of lead and copper.

"I find you bastards and I cut your fucking hearts out and I eat them. I eat them! You can wander in the damn dark with no hearts."

He sat on the hood of his cruiser.

He rolled a smoke and lit it and inhaled and he coughed and coughed.

151

My throat is raw from that yelling, Du Pré thought. I have some whiskey. I am drinking too much. Too much is when you like it too much. Better not do it so much, it don't damp no fires. Make them hotter.

Madelaine is half-crazy with fear, her babies get killed, this man. Du Pré had some whiskey.

He looked up at the rim three hundred feet above.

He dropped the bottle on the ground.

He got a canteen from the trunk and he put it on, the strap over his shoulder, diagonal to his body.

He began to walk up the trail he could see, a white snake moving among the sagebrush.

He scrambled and cursed up the steep places. Put his hands where he shouldn't, rattlesnakes might lie up there on the warm rocks.

Fucking snake bite me I am so mad it *die*.

Hunt these guys.

Can't kill them, that Harvey is not kidding.

Neither am I.

Du Pré tore his hand open on a sharp rock. He sucked blood from the deep gash. He looked down. Obsidian spearpoint sticking out of the yellow earth, thin and settled between two rocks. Du Pré tugged at it. It would not come. He pulled his folding tool from his belt and got the screwdriver blade out and he dug away.

Stuck through a bone. Clear through it.

Buffalo rib bone. Bull die all the way up here.

Why they bother to kill it?

Du Pré looked up at the rim. He was centered under it.

Shaman was under it, that's why.

Du Pré got hold of the rib bone and he heaved. It came free. The rib suddenly split open and the spearpoint fell. Du Pré caught it in the air.

Du Pré held the black volcanic glass up to his eyes.

The stars glittered in the conchoidal fractures.

Knapper, he move around the edge with an elk tine.

Du Pré sat a moment.

He looked down at his cruiser. A coyote was walking past the front of it, and the coyote stopped and pissed.

"Yes, my friend," laughed Du Pré.

Benetsee.

✤ CHAPTER 32 ✤

Du Pré was eating breakfast with his left hand. His right palm had thirty stitches in it and it hurt like hell. He mashed a piece of ham apart with his fork and he put it in his mouth.

Madelaine sat across the table. She had eaten a bite of an egg. She was smoking one of the tailor-made cigarettes Du Pré had bought in Miles City. She was drinking coffee. Her eyes had dark circles under them and she was edgy.

"You are not talking to your Madelaine these days, Du Pré," she said. "You go off someplace, come back with them funny clothes, go off again, come back with your hand cut open bad. You don't say nothin'. You know who this guy is. I know it. You don't talk to me."

Damn right, Du Pré thought, you go on the warpath and cut off that Simpson's balls I let you know who I think it is, he is. Then Harvey he get to arrest you. I don't think so.

"What you find where you went?" She was looking at him very hard.

"Not much," said Du Pré. He bent his head and he strained to crush another piece of ham away from the steak.

"You are not talking to me, Du Pré," said Madelaine.

Christ, thought Du Pré, I had better lie some, I guess. But she will know I am lying.

Du Pré shrugged.

Madelaine dashed her coffee in his face.

153

"You know this guy is!" she yelled. Then she threw a plate of corn muffins at him and she jumped up and began to fire all of the dishes in the drainer.

Du Pré dropped down below the table.

She pegged crockery at him between the legs.

"Jesus, Mama!" said Cyrill, her youngest. "You are crazy!"

"Fucking bastard Métis son of a bitch cocksucker," screamed Madelaine.

Du Pré hunkered. If he ran she'd chase him. Might as well confine the damage to the one room.

Cyrill ran off.

Du Pré wished him a long life in a dark hole.

Madelaine nailed Du Pré on the left knee with a big crockery bowl.

"Ah!" said Du Pré. "I am dead. You have killed me!"

"My fucking cousin's baby she is dead with her head cut off and you won't talk to me!" yelled Madelaine. She was down to silverware.

Du Pré tried to remember if there were any big sharp knives in the drainer. He couldn't.

A big sharp knife stuck in the floor in front of his leg. It thunked when it hit and it quivered.

"Jesus!" said Du Pré. "I am finding this guy, you know, you want to kill me before I do?"

"Bastard!" yelled Madelaine.

"People, people," said Father Van Den Heuvel, rushing in the front door. "Please! Madelaine! Gabriel!"

The big priest slipped on the hall runner and he crashed into the glass-fronted cabinet that held Madelaine's collection of porcelain. The sound of the collision was awful.

"Oh," said Madelaine.

"Oh," said Du Pré.

"SHIT!" said Father Van Den Heuvel.

Madelaine was still.

Then she began to laugh, low and throaty. She went on.

Du Pré peeked over the top of the table at her. She was looking at him and laughing and shaking her head.

Father Van Den Heuvel crunched to his feet. He began to brush little white shards of porcelain from his cassock.

"Men," said Madelaine. Her voice was thick with amused contempt.

Du Pré stood up and he looked around the kitchen at all the damage. Couple holes in the plaster walls he would now get to patch. Have to drive Madelaine all the damn way to Billings, get new crockery. He measured the distance between where the knife hit and where his nuts had been sitting. Less than a foot.

Du Pré was a very smart man. He kept his mouth shut.

"I'm . . . very . . . sorry," stammered the priest. He had little bits of glass and porcelain on his black robe.

"Shit . . . heads," said Madelaine, laughing.

Du Pré nodded vigorously and kept quiet.

"I'll buy you some new . . ." said the priest lamely.

"Oh, no," said Madelaine. "You do not. You were trying to help. Me, I lose my temper, God punish me. He also forgive me right away, you guys are such assholes. I watch you, years, you do these things, mostly us women we just smile and shrug. You can't help it, them two heads, always thinkin' with the little one. Priests, too. Father crap you talk. Me, I pray to Mother of God. He needs one. Fucking fools. You men. Bah."

When Madelaine got mad her eyes flashed crimson on the black irises. Lots of Assiniboine blood in her. Women famous for their beauty, famous for their tempers, famous for being very warlike.

Wonder them damn Assiniboines don't run about everybody up a tree, Du Pré thought, women like these in the camp. Jesus.

"Well," said Father Van Den Heuvel, "now that we are all calm . . ."

"Me, I am not calm," said Madelaine. "I am not calm. You are just so sorry I cannot help but laugh. My niece she is lying dead, head cut off and stuck in her belly. No, I am not calm a little. Fucking Du Pré he go off looking, that guy, some guy, he don't find nothing,

155

dumb shit he still come home. You know what we do, days of the carts?"

Du Pré kept his mouth shut.

"Carts?" said Father Van Den Heuvel.

"Long time," said Madelaine. "You guys you aren't much around, come, help make a baby, we send you off, be a voyageur, a hunter, 'cept for those of you supposed to be ten miles away from the camp make sure nothing get to us and our babies."

Du Pré nodded.

"So I am mad," said Madelaine.

Du Pré nodded.

"Du Pré he knows something and he will not tell me. He will not tell me because he does not want, scare this guy. He rather scare me instead. Don't let me know, maybe use one of my babies as some bait."

Du Pré shook his head.

"Shit," said Madelaine. "You lie to me, Du Pré. I cut your damn dick off right then."

Du Pré looked at the ceiling.

"We must be gentle with each other," said the priest.

"You shove up your ass, gentle with each other," said Madelaine. "That damn Du Pré know someone he think maybe do this and he won't tell me so it don't scare the guy off. He don't trust me."

No shit, thought Du Pré, you take a shotgun to him, be sure that it not come from his direction. No shit I don't tell you.

"Uh," said Father Van Den Heuvel. "We could go and get a cup of coffee and maybe talk."

"Priest," said Madelaine, "I want shit out of you I squeeze your head. My baby Lourdes we are talking, my baby Simone. You think more people save this damn Du Pré's sorry ass I think maybe you squeeze your own head. Now, you are nice man, but you are not much help. Why don't you go, talk to someone, listens. I got no time."

"Uh," said Father Van Den Heuvel.

"You go," said Du Pré. "You go on. She is right."

"Please," said the priest. "No more of this."

"More of what?" said Madelaine. "I bust up some, cheap Kmart

156

plates, bowls, you wipe out all my porcelain, some my great-grandmother's. Some help."

"I'll go," said Father Van Den Heuvel.

"In some time I be sorry I am mean to you," said Madelaine, "but now I am not sorry. Go talk, someone else. Go fuck a goddamn goat. Go fuck a goddamn goat in your church, there, I got to talk, this Métis piece of shit."

Du Pré held his hands up, palms to the sky. He looked at the priest and he shrugged.

"You got to go," said Du Pré. "Me, I maybe die but you cannot help that either."

"He give you that Extreme Unction," said Madelaine.

"I . . ." said the priest. He was almost gasping.

"It will be all right," said Du Pré. "People, they die all the time. It is very common thing for them to do."

"I say I am sorry, I won't throw nothing more at Du Pré. I not cut his damn nuts off. I am sorry my Jesus. I lose my temper, I come say your fucking Hail Marys and I repent a lot when I fucking well want to repent," said Madelaine. "But you better go now."

The big priest crunched away on the bones of Madelaine's porcelain. The door shut gently.

They heard a yelp when he tripped and fell off the porch.

They waited.

The car door slammed. The car started.

"Him," said Madelaine. "At least he don't shut his head in it this time."

Du Pré nodded.

"I find the guy, I am following him," said Du Pré.

"He in my kitchen, here?" said Madelaine.

"I got to go," said Du Pré.

"Yah," said Madelaine. "You better, better not come back he is dead, you hear me?"

Du Pré nodded.

"My babies," said Madelaine.

Du Pré left.

❖ CHAPTER 33 ❖

Du Pré was sleeping on a high ridge that reached out west from the Wolf Mountains. He'd found a place with several stone peekaboos, piles of flat plates of shale left long ago by other hunters. They could look through the gaps between the stones and not show any movement. From the ridge, Du Pré could see maybe seventy miles north and a hundred west and fifty south. To the east the Wolf Mountains rose, stacked in an east–west line, blue flanks of pine and spruce and fir, the rock above the timberline gray as the sea, some snow on the peaks every month of the year.

A mule deer, curious, had come to look at him. The deer slipped on some shattered yellow mudstones and it leaped in panic and sent down a shower of rock from the ledge it climbed in one bound. Du Pré awoke, his gun in his hand.

There was a flash of green light. A meteor streaked yellow-green across the sky, north to south. The bright trail faded quickly. Du Pré shut his eyes and the dancing spot where the last yellow flash as the meteor evaporated utterly burned a moment behind his eyes.

It was cold. The wind was still. The air was dry.

My people come down from Red River in the fall, Du Pré thought, to get that winter meat. Drive them little two-wheeled Red River carts, cottonwood rounds for wheels, not a piece of metal in them, they carry the parfleches, we drive the buffalo into corrals and kill them, dry the meat, the leader of the hunt he makes sure everybody got all their winter meat before he take any. Go on home. Them Sioux, Assiniboine, Blackfeet, sometimes the Crows they try to steal our horses, steal our women, kill the men, drive us away from the buffalo. We don't go. We got them Hudson's Bay Company muskets.

Trail is right over there ten miles. No Red River carts, long time. I can still hear them, the night. Screek screek screek, you hear them axles, twenty miles across the prairies. No grease on them, time to time, they catch fire. Métis men, they piss on them, keep them cool. Not so much water here.

Red River.

Benetsee and Madelaine they tell me things, better listen.

That Bart, I go to him, say, I need someone, keep on that Simpson's trail, keep real close. So that Bart, he look at me, see his chance. If he got someone close, I don't kill that damn Simpson.

Some reporter, Bart's newspapers, he is with that crew, big story in the Sunday paper, "Do You Know Where Your Noodles Come From?"

That Hi-Line Killer, him I got to find.

Dream that deer and the deer come.

Dream that killer and he leave me a track.

Sick bastard.

Du Pré slid out of his bedroll and he walked a few feet away and he pissed. The stream steamed in the cold night air.

OK, my Madelaine, I am out, the country, keep him away from you, your babies. Like we used to do. Don't paint my face, though.

It was four in the morning. The dawn would come in an hour, a first faint rim of pink in the east.

Du Pré rolled up his blankets and sougans in his henskin and he fastened the clips and he tossed it to his shoulder and he walked down to where his old cruiser was parked. He dropped the bedroll into the trunk and he set the bag with his whiskey and tobacco and spare 9mm clips and ammunition and jerky and chocolate on the front seat. He had turned the car around when he had parked it. He drove down the rutted stony trail to the county road, followed that to a small two-lane blacktop. The road was narrow and poorly surfaced. Du Pré sped along at seventy-five, wallowing around the worst potholes.

He got to Raster Creek's rest area when the light was rising to full day. He parked the cruiser and went into the john and came back out and he walked slowly back to where little Barbara Morissette had lain, her head stuck in her belly and the flies dancing around the blood and wounds.

He took his time.

Some guy, walked back here, maybe yesterday, the afternoon. Du Pré got down on his haunches and he looked at the faint print of a bootsole, a hiking boot with five stars up the center of the sole.

He counted the ant tracks across the earth. Into the faint depression and on toward whatever it was that the ants were working on. A bombardier beetle had scuttled across. Four and one. He looked over at the anthill twenty feet away.

Yah, he thought, maybe twenty-four hours. Less, I think. Yesterday afternoon, late. No dew, no rain. Who are you?

He looked ahead at the line of tracks going straight to where little Barbara had lain. No dog tracks, the guy wasn't pumping his pooch out. He was going right there. No reason to go right there. No reason . . .

Du Pré went on. He saw a folded piece of yellow paper, one the size of a deck of cards. Thirty feet ahead.

Du Pré moved slower than he had.

Same tracks. Don't miss nothing now.

The piece of paper had got stuck against a sagebrush. Little wind did that. Yesterday late afternoon, when the wind always comes up from the west.

Du Pré moved slowly.

When he got to the paper he squatted and he reached out and picked it up gently and he turned it over in his fingers. The paper was crushed and shiny and on one side there was a faint stain, a brown one. Guy folded it, stuck it in his hip pocket between his wallet and his ass. Sat on it. Sweated in it. Tamped it down good.

Du Pré looked up at a hawk that had floated between Du Pré and the rising sun. The shadow had flitted across his face. The hawk was hovering. It plunged and Du Pré heard a squeak, cut off.

Du Pré unfolded the paper. Heavy, yellow stock. Printed with an announcement for a model airplane show. In Fargo, North Dakota. In two days.

Du Pré looked at the other side.

A name. An address. In Renton, Washington.

Du Pré looked at it for a long time.

He refolded the paper and he put it in his pocket and he went on toward little Barbara Morissette's killing ground.

Du Pré saw the cheap pair of girl's underwear cast on the ground where Barbara had lain. He went forward quickly and he picked up the panties and he saw the stains on them. He looked down and there were the spread prints of the bootsoles and the little gouge where a heavy belt buckle had hit to the left of the left foot when the man had dropped his pants to jerk off.

Only this guy, Du Pré thought, is him. Nobody else been back here. Just this guy. He was here, not long ago.

Du Pré walked back quickly to his cruiser. He stuffed the panties into the trash receptacle, down under a bag of cans and cigarette butts. He took out the yellow piece of paper and he stared at it for a long time.

Then he struck a farmer's match and he burned it and he ground the black ash to smears on the yellow earth.

OK, I come now.

Du Pré looked toward the sun in the east. It was shining red through low haze.

Du Pré got in his cruiser. He rolled a smoke and he had a little whiskey. He was thirsty. He got some big glasses of cold water from a blue-and-white thermal jug. He ate a little jerky.

He drove on east. Fast. He got to a junction and he angled off south a little. He drove like hell. He got to the Interstate and he got on and he slowed down twenty miles an hour.

He stopped and got gas just over the line in North Dakota. He passed the place where the Yellowstone and Missouri Rivers joined.

Used to be a big trading post there.

Take them furs in, get bad whiskey. Trade beads, knives, brass pots and vermilion, needles and thread, flour, tobacco.

Voyageurs, some of them take the boats down to St. Louis, New Orleans. Float down, haul them damn boats back up on a rope over your shoulder. Long damn walk. Takes two years, the trip back.

Du Pré turned off on a secondary highway and he headed toward the Turtle Mountain Reservation.

Been many times, this country, he thought.

See them cousins of mine.

Talk to Bassman.

Du Pré called Bassman's house from a pay phone at a gas station.

The number was temporarily out of service.

'Nother poor Métis, can't pay his phone bill.

Du Pré drove on to Bassman's house. His first wife had got drunk and died in a car wreck five years ago. Bassman had remarried quickly and the kids from the first and second marriages were all playing in the yard, a year or so between their ages. Except that there wasn't a four-year-old, since Bassman had taken ten months or a year to find that new wife. The kids were running around and laughing and the older ones were watching out for the younger ones. A couple disreputable yellow dogs barked when Du Pré pulled in and he parked.

Bassman came out the front door. He was wearing a tattered red T-shirt, jeans, and moccasins. His hair was braided. This month, he was Indian. Next month, maybe, he cut his hair short and wear a long-sleeved Western shirt, hide the needle tracks on his arms. Bassman had spent ten years in LA, mostly not very good ones.

Du Pré liked him a lot.

"Du Pré," said Bassman, "you come on in here, now, you eat?"

"Yah," said Du Pré.

"You look tired. Sleep?"

Du Pré shook his head.

"Ah," said Bassman, coming down to the cluttered yard. "You need a car got them good North Dakota license plates."

Du Pré nodded. Moccasin telegraph still worked pretty good.

"I got you a good one," said Bassman.

They drove over to where it was. Pretty new van, good engine, good tires. Dark blue. Curtain behind the bucket seats.

"Keys in it," said Bassman, carrying Du Pré's bedroll. "All gassed, you need anything, Fargo, you call that Le Bon. Toussaint Le Bon. He fiddles some good as you."

Du Pré nodded. He lifted his bag from the front seat of the cruiser.

He walked to the van and he got in and he tossed his bag on the floor behind.

He rolled down the window.

Bassman handed him a paper bag. It had something small and heavy in it. It rattled a little.

Du Pré looked at Bassman.

Bassman nodded.

✤ CHAPTER 34 ✤

Du Pré was filthy. He hadn't shaved and he reeked of sweat and cheap wine.

The fairgrounds had a big crowd of people in it, all come to see the model airplane show. The little planes zoomed and snarled and dived and the operators stood in little knots watching the competition.

Du Pré had taken one pass through the parking area and he found the truck he was looking for. A van, long-bed, dusty from the long drive. The rear tires were larger than the ones on the front. They were radials and they were deformed. The van was heavier in the rear than it should be. Du Pré glanced in the rear window. The floor was elevated a foot and a half from the original. Du Pré walked around the driver's side. There was an extra gas cap and it was mounted high, back of the driver's door. The other was behind a locking flap.

Washington plates.

Du Pré straightened up and he walked to a trash bin and tossed in the bottle of cheap wine in its brown paper bag. He walked to the van Bassman had found for him and he got in and he shaved and washed up and put on the loud tropical shirt that he had bought in Miles City and the pants and running shoes. He scribbled on a piece of paper and tucked it in the pocket of his shirt. He went to the registry booth and handed the paper to a woman, who was looking at someone else. Du Pré slid away rapidly. He went back to the van with the Washington plates and past it to a pile of railroad ties left for some future corral construction and he sat down and rolled a smoke.

The public address system bellowed the name that he had found on the yellow sheet of paper, and said that there was some trouble with his van.

In three minutes a tall, thin man with the long arms and ropy muscles of a stevedore or a choker setter came loping across the parking lot. He had long stringy blond hair. He wore jeans and running shoes and a sweatshirt. The sweatshirt hung down over his belt.

Du Pré looked at him.

Well, well.

Du Pré waited till the man had given up in the matter of his car and a problem and he went back toward the field where the little planes were taking off and landing.

Du Pré sauntered after him.

The man joined two others who were fussing over a model Piper Cub, checking the actions of the little joystick on the control box with the flaps and ailerons on the model plane.

One of the two men squatting on the ground spun the propellor with his finger and the little engine caught and the plane quivered while the tiny motor spat and banged.

The man Du Pré was after stood back. He wasn't with these two, just watching.

One of the two took the plane out to the dirt runway and held it while the operator revved the engine and then gave the thumbs-up. The man holding the plane let go and the little plane dashed down the dirt and lifted easily into the air and it flew almost straight up.

When the little plane came down the man Du Pré was after made some remark and the two men at the control box looked at him and they didn't laugh. The man colored and he turned quickly and walked away toward a block building that had rest rooms in it.

He was in there a long time.

When he came out he blinked at the bright sun for a while. He went off toward one of the fair barns.

Du Pré followed him as he went around the displays of kits and engines and paints, fabrics and plans, the skeletal assemblies of models awaiting the silk coverings and the coats of varnish.

The man paused at a booth that held replicas of WW II fighters. The details were fine and well wrought and the man spent an hour talking with the builder. The builder was getting exasperated with him, because he would not move out of the way and let others look, too. Finally the seller had enough and told the man to move on.

This guy is not right, Du Pré thought.

I knew that.

The man spent the next two hours wandering and staring at the displays. Du Pré did, too, following at a distance.

The crowd began to stream through the doors and out to the field. The public address system announced a dogfight between an American plane and a Japanese Zero. Du Pré went, too, staying a hundred feet or so behind the man he was after. The man stopped.

Du Pré moved back on a line between the man and the van with the Washington plates.

The dogfight started. The little planes snarled and climbed and went through corkscrews and did Immelmann turns and they each fired little fake machine guns.

The crowd watched the planes and Du Pré watched the man.

The man began to move back toward Du Pré.

Du Pré rolled a cigarette.

He passed thirty feet from Du Pré and he went between the parked cars toward his own van. He was hurrying.

Du Pré followed.

The crowd was all staring up at the two little planes.

When the man got to his van he went around to the back and he was opening the door to get in when Du Pré stepped out and shot him twice in the head with a small .22 pistol that had a perforated silencer made out of aluminum pipe on the end of it.

The gun went phut phut and the man Du Pré was after straightened up and then he fell into the van. He was dead. Du Pré shoved his legs in and he tossed the gun after him and he peeled off the plastic painting glove he had on his right hand and he stuffed it in his pocket. He shut the door and he wiped the handle with his kerchief.

Du Pré walked through the parked cars to the van he had borrowed and he got in and he drove slowly away.

The crowd sent up a loud cheer. The Zero was trailing a plume of black smoke.

Du Pré turned out of the fairgrounds and he got on the expressway and drove and drove until he felt hungry. He stopped in Bismarck and went to a good restaurant and he ate a big steak and two slices of apple pie with ice cream.

Du Pré got gas and he stopped at a liquor store and got a pint of bourbon and he drove till three in the morning. When he pulled into Bassman's yard the lights came on briefly in the house and then Bassman came out with a couple men that Du Pré had met years before but he couldn't remember whether or not they played music.

One of the men got in the van and he helped pass out Du Pré's stuff and Du Pré stuck his bedroll back in the trunk of the cruiser and then he took his bag and set that on the driver's seat.

The two men with Bassman left in the van Du Pré had used.

Bassman brought out a big plate of sausages and cheese and cold cuts and vegetables and a jug of cheap wine and they ate silently sitting on Bassman's little porch with the half-moon up above.

Du Pré got his fiddle and Bassman got a guitar out of the house and they sat and played some old music.

They played "Baptiste's Lament." They played some shanties and some meat songs. They played a couple songs the voyageurs sang after they had carried the heavy packs of furs around a hard portage.

After a while, they just sat and drank and smoked.

166

"I will be over, there," said Bassman. "Maybe a month, we play that good music, that bar. Me, I like that woman who own it. You know, she give us each a hundred dollars last time we play there?"

Du Pré nodded. Susan wouldn't insult him by offering to pay him, but she knew that Bassman and musicians like him never had any money. They spent it all on pretty women and booze and silk shirts and strings for their instruments.

"Yeah," said Du Pré. "She is a good person."

"Your Madelaine, she is well?" said Bassman. His eyes were twinkling.

"She is plenty good," said Du Pré.

"She dance real good," said Bassman.

"Yes," said Du Pré.

"When you maybe come back here to Turtle Mountain," said Bassman, "we maybe play some music, the bars here."

"I like that," said Du Pré.

"You play that good Métis music," said Bassman. "You know them young people used to think we were shit, they are coming around now, saying, hey, you teach me the old music. I thought they all would maybe like that Michael Jackson or something. But they are working good at it. I got a couple kids, one of them plays the fiddle, they be pret' good ten years or so."

"Take a long time," said Du Pré.

He looked up at the stars, at the Drinking Gourd that pointed to the Pole Star.

Long time ago, my grandpère he give me a little fiddle, I am maybe eight or something. I make noise. My grandpère he smile and say I do good. Catfoot, he play and I drive him crazy.

They teach me a long time. Get me a couple more fiddles.

One I got now was grandpère's. Had to get a little work done on it but it sounds right.

Play them old songs.

Didn't play really well until my wife she die. I play all right before she die, but better after, I am very sad.

Maybe you got to lose something big, play well.

What have I lost, maybe?

Du Pré put his fiddle in the case.

"I got to go home," he said.

Bassman nodded. He held out his hand.

"You come back, Du Pré," he said. "We play that good music."

❧ CHAPTER 35 ❧

Rolly Challis looked at the little black receiving unit. Du Pré stood with his arms folded and he waited.

"Looks good," said Rolly. "If you can do your end. Three days. Day after tomorrow after tomorrow. Works out good. I can make it to Spokane and then on and back, no problem."

Du Pré nodded.

Rolly grinned at him and he got up in his big black semi and pulled out on Highway 2 and headed west.

Du Pré went to a picnic table and he sat on it for a while and had a smoke and then he got in his cruiser and headed south.

The Wolf Mountains rose on his left.

Shit hit the fan pret' soon, Du Pré thought. Maybe. All I need, them FBI got somebody following that asshole I killed in Fargo. They are not maybe that smart.

Oh, bullshit, I would have been arrested, my way out of the fairgrounds. There is no one there. I would have seen them.

Not my kind of work.

It is now.

If that was the guy. If not, he still maybe should not jerk off over where little Barbara she is left dead, her head in her belly.

Tracks. That was the track, yes.

That Harvey, he add it up, be all over me like stink on shit anyway. I can hear him. Me, I just ask him he want another drink, otherwise, you fuck off maybe.

One more.

That Madelaine, I miss her but I am not going home until I am done. She is not, any mood, half the job done.

I think.

When did this all start?

Red River.

You are a poor Métis, you had better take care, your life.

Live my life under them Wolf Mountains. On these High Plains. On what was Red River.

Sometimes, I wish my people beat them English. Have our own country.

English they are pret' smart and mean as hell, nobody beat them.

Du Pré reached under the seat and he took the bottle and he had a snort. The whiskey made him cough a little. It burned good.

Du Pré rocketed down the highway. It was a clear late summer day and the air was clean. It had rained some in the night. Enough to knock the dust down. The western horizon was gray with more.

When Du Pré got to Toussaint it was early in the day. He parked in front of the bar and he went on in. The place smelled of bleach and cleanser and polish. Susan kept it scrubbed. She had hired two women to help her three days a week plus Sunday morning.

She looked up when Du Pré came in, and then she ducked down again.

Du Pré leaned over the counter.

She was inside one of the coolers, scrubbing.

"Make yourself whatever," she said.

Du Pré came round the bar and mixed himself a ditch.

"Your pal Harvey," she said, "called for you. He sounded pissed."

"Them Blackfeet, they are pissed all their life," said Du Pré.

"Yeah," said Susan. "Well, he was so pissed he said that he was going to be here soon to be pissed at you personally."

"Check I give him, it bounce," said Du Pré.

"Yeah," said Susan. "You been gone a while. Madelaine has come in here looking for you a couple a times."

The cooler made her voice big.

"She got a gun, knife, she come in?" said Du Pré.

"No," said Susan. "You ain't been pronging one of those women make the eyes at you when you play, have you?"

"Which women?" said Du Pré.

"Damn near all of them, you Métis son of a bitch," said Susan. "I didn't love Benny so much I'd jump your bones myself. You are a pretty man and you play real good."

"I don't love nobody, Madelaine," said Du Pré.

"I thought so," said Susan Klein, "but, then, you are a guy, and you guys got such strange notions of what you can do and live."

"I help you any?" said Du Pré.

"Guys," said Susan, "cannot clean anything for sour owlshit. You lugs are like bears with furniture. Benny tries to help me clean. He does the bathroom. He really works at it. Always looks worse than before he tried. You guys are pathetic."

Du Pré nodded at himself in the mirror.

"What'd you and Madelaine fight about?" said Susan.

"I don't know," said Du Pré.

"I bet you don't," said Susan. "I really do." She got out of the cooler and she stood up. She was flushed and sweaty. She had a blue bandanna around her head. Her work shirt was stained dark under the arms.

"You oughta call her," said Susan.

Du Pré looked down at his drink.

"OK," said Susan. "I will." She went to the phone and she dialed.

Du Pré sat on a barstool. He felt sick.

Madelaine came right away. She walked up to the bar and she slid up on a stool and Susan poured her a glass of the sweet, bubbly pink wine she liked. Then Susan went off through the door to the storeroom in back.

"Hey, Du Pré," said Madelaine, "you been gone, long time, don't call your Madelaine. What is her name, this new one."

Du Pré looked at her.

She dropped her eyes.

"OK," she said. "I am sorry. I am sorry for all of this."

"Well," said Du Pré, "I am not liking it much."

"Where you been?" she said.

Du Pré shrugged.

"Oh," said Madelaine, "you did that."

Du Pré looked at the mirror. He felt like he was going to puke.

"Is this, over?" said Madelaine.

Du Pré shook his head.

"OK," said Madelaine. "I don't ask you no more dumb questions."

Du Pré felt sick. He ran to the men's room. The door was open. The place was freshly mopped. He puked in the toilet, bent over and heaving. He retched and retched till he was pale and shaking and running sweat. He stood over the sink for a while, his hands on it, then he ran cold water and he scrubbed his face and splashed it on his neck. He dried off with wads of paper towels.

He went back out.

Madelaine was standing there, she was holding a bottle of the whiskey that he liked.

"You come home," said Madelaine. "You have not been eating right. You need a bath, maybe three. You come home, let your Madelaine take care of you. You come now."

Du Pré went out and he opened the door of the cruiser for her and she got in and he drove to her place.

Madelaine led him inside. She made him a hot strong toddy with lemon and sugar and whiskey and he drank it down all at once. She cooked some mild sausage and rice. He ate. He had two more toddies.

He went off and stood in the shower for an hour, the steaming water sluicing over him.

Never wash this off, he thought.

What am I ashamed of?

He got angry. The water turned cooler. Du Pré shut off the valves and he got out and toweled himself and he went to Madelaine's room. There were clean clothes on the bed. He got dressed and he went out to the kitchen. The back door was open. He went out and found Madelaine sitting at the picnic table under the little bower covered with hop vines. She had a pitcher of pale brown liquid and ice with her.

She was rolling Du Pré some cigarettes.

Du Pré went and he sat down beside her.

He lit a smoke.

"OK," said Madelaine. "Now you are mad at yourself some, kill that guy."

"What guy?" said Du Pré, angrily.

"I only say this once," said Madelaine. "I never talk about that guy you killed again. You going to kill the other one, too. Thank you, they killing people's babies, have, long time."

Du Pré poured himself a drink. He drank. His mouth tasted all right again.

"You are a good man, Du Pré. You maybe have to do bad things because of bad men, these cops, they never catch these guys, you know. They have not, how long, twenty years?"

Du Pré lit another cigarette.

"You are a real gentle man, Du Pré," said Madelaine. "You don't like this at all. If you did, I would not love you. I would not. Men who like it are not right, you know."

Du Pré sipped his drink.

"But you do what you have to," said Madelaine. "I am proud of you and I don't talk, this, again."

Du Pré nodded.

"You going to be a long time, getting over," said Madelaine. "Don't get over all of it, ever. Life, it is not nice. Sometimes."

Du Pré looked at her.

"Now," said Madelaine, "that Blackfeet Harvey he is pissed, he is coming here. I not say anything, you don't, that is all."

"So you get some rest now. I fix you a good supper."

Du Pré nodded.

He went in to sleep.

He lay there a long time before he drifted off.

✤ CHAPTER 36 ✤

Harvey and Pidgeon sat on one side of the table and Du Pré sat on the other. They had legal tablets in front of them and tape recorders. They were wearing Bureau drag.

Du Pré was in faded denim and he had a sack of Bull Durham and some papers and his shepherd's lighter.

"No smoking," said Harvey.

"Kiss my ass," said Du Pré.

"This isn't funny, guys," said Pidgeon.

"It's not a formal interrogation," said Harvey.

"No shit," said Pidgeon.

"You piss me off, Du Pré," said Harvey.

"You guys want me to leave so you can just lock antlers and have a good old time pawing the fucking earth I will," said Pidgeon.

"Humor me," said Harvey.

"Kiss my ass," said Pidgeon.

"Look, Pidgeon," said Harvey, "I need to do this. Our leading suspect ends up dead in fucking Fargo, North Dakota, with small slugs in his head. Looks like a standard biker hit. But nobody was mad at him. Our snitches don't have a clue. Old Larry had nothing but friends, all of whom thought he was weird. You ever deal with this fucker across the table before?"

"Perfect gentleman," said Pidgeon.

"Du Pré," said Harvey, "you will answer my questions."

"No," said Du Pré.

"I oughta demand you take another lie detector test," said Harvey.

"Kiss my ass," said Du Pré.

"Look, Harvey," said Pidgeon, "we got things like rules, you know, the old indictment, the arrest, the eyewitness, the evidence, all that shit. You get something, we could do this, but you got nothing and we all know it. If fucking Du Pré waxed the cocksucker he did a nice clean job. What? You just want to come out here, shoot some grouse or something?"

"I am your superior," snarled Harvey.

"Be still my pattering itty-bitty heart," said Pidgeon. "You want to rag on Gabriel you go right ahead, you want to fire me just try it. I'll have you up on harassment charges, your hand on my ass and all."

"I have never put my hand on your ass," said Harvey.

"I got some bad news for you," said Pidgeon. "Jury takes one look at my ass and they just will not believe any guy could help himself. Little perjury on my part, Harvey, it's a tough world out there. Now, we are all just mammals tryin' to make it in a hostile universe but, really, you want to get on Du Pré's ass maybe you just oughta go out, the parking lot and duke it out. I will take these here tape recorders, but the good news is I am destroying these tapes." She stuffed both of them in her attaché case, after taking the cassettes out and putting them in her bra. She rebuttoned her white silk blouse. High.

Harvey broke a pencil in half.

"I don't think he's gettin' enough at home," said Pidgeon. "As a psychologist, I can tell you the world runs on pussy or the lack of it."

"Pidgeon," said Harvey, "enough. You're a bad little girl. Act your fucking age."

"Studies have shown," said Pidgeon, "that they show things. This is a perfect example of what it is. Now, what have we really got . . . ?"

"This bastard Simpson," said Harvey.

"Oh, yes," said Pidgeon. "Now, we're talkin'. I *like* Simpson. He is a *fave*. I give him the *big* 10. Wish I had some *evidence*, though."

"Oh, that," said Harvey.

"Yeah," said Pidgeon. "I mean, I just can't see a judge, no matter how stupid, giving us a warrant. Can't see a grand jury of all them good citizens listening to us say, Simpson's a *fave*, the murdering bastard of all time. We all think so. Don't have a single shred of evidence, though, you'll have to take our hunches."

"However," said Harvey, "I would like Du Pré to know that if, say, the fave Simpson should be hit by lightning, I cannot help myself. I will wonder if Du Pré was sitting there next to the switch."

"Oh, 'tis true," said Pidgeon. "We got spy satellites hovering overhead and they take nifty photos. Get a snapshot of old Du Pré punching the fave Simpson's ticket, we will have to fry our friend here. We got little microphones in Simpson's jockstrap. We got undercover agents cleverly disguised as spare tires in that van of his. We got him *locked.*"

Du Pré rolled a smoke.

"Pidgeon," said Harvey, "you really ought to be nicer. It's a good thing to be nice. I am nice, too. I am nicely trying to explain to this fucking prairie nigger across the table here that I am worried that I will have to arrest him and send him to Walla Walla."

"Prairie nigger?" said Pidgeon. "I think that means Indian? My Cherokee blood cries out for justice. Shame on you. We got a Blackfeet, a Creek Cherokee White Negro, a Cree Chippewa Frog. All in this room, right here. Du Pré, Harvey's gone round the bend. His cake fell. His elevator is stuck between floors. His bread ain't baked. His deck is short of jacks. Racial slurs. Tsk tsk."

Harvey reached over and he got Du Pré's tobacco and papers and he rolled a smoke.

"Me, too," said Pidgeon. She took Harvey's.

"So," said Harvey, "I ever tell you about Du Pré and his machine gun?"

"No," said Pidgeon. "You have seen this machine gun?"

"No," said Harvey. "I heard it once."

"Harvey," said Pidgeon, "if you didn't see the fucking machine gun, or pick up brass can be *matched* to it, or *slugs*, all you did was hear it, maybe all you heard was regrettable flatulence."

"Look," said Du Pré, "I am wanting to maybe go back down to the bar and maybe play some pool or something."

"Hooray," said Pidgeon.

"Think we're ready for prime time?" said Harvey.

Du Pré grinned.

"Of course we are, Harvey," said Pidgeon, "but first, let us tell the good Mr. Du Pré that Simpson is indeed about to be arrested, by God, and real soon."

Du Pré sat up.

"So we'd just as soon he didn't fuck us up," said Harvey.

"It would be nice," said Pidgeon.

"You got something?" said Du Pré.

"*That*," said Harvey, "we can't talk about."

"Nope," said Pidgeon. "We can't, at all."

"How good it is?" said Du Pré.

"Fair," said Harvey.

"So, hands off," said Pidgeon. "I mean it."

Du Pré shrugged.

"Really," said Harvey.

Du Pré stood up.

"I got shoot some pool," he said. "Keeps my eye in."

"Bully idea," said Pidgeon.

"Cheeseburger," said Harvey.

They left the trailer behind Susan Klein's Toussaint Bar and they went in the back door. The day was chilly enough so that Susan had lit a small fire in the woodstove. Pidgeon tossed the cassettes in on the red coals.

Du Pré got a drink and he went over to the pool table and he put two quarters in the slots and dropped the balls out of the belly. He racked and set them and he took the cueball and went to the other end and he set the ball and broke the rack smoothly. Two balls went in.

Harvey was talking to Susan Klein.

Pidgeon was squinting down a cue. She nodded finally and she put five dollars on the side of the table and looked at Du Pré.

Du Pré nodded and he matched her bet.

Pidgeon nodded and ran all the stripes into pockets without pause and then she picked one for the eight ball and sank it.

She picked up the two fives.

Du Pré nodded.

She put them back down.

Du Pré nodded.

She broke and nothing went in.

Du Pré ran six and then he fluffed a bank shot.

Pidgeon mercilessly cleared the table.

When the bet topped two hundred and Du Pré still hadn't come close to winning, Pidgeon grinned and nodded again.

There were ten or so people standing around looking on now. Making side bets. Harvey had money but not one taker on his player. Pidgeon, of course.

"How about five hundred?" said Pidgeon.

Du Pré nodded.

Du Pré chalked his cue tip and he smiled and then he bent down and ran the table.

He picked up the thousand dollars.

Pidgeon nodded.

She kissed him on the cheek.

"It was him," she whispered. "We found all sorts of stuff in the van."

❧ CHAPTER 37 ❧

H e's headed south," said the voice.
Du Pré hung the telephone up.

That Simpson, back home to Texas again.

Like hell.

Bart sipped his tea. He was wearing irrigation boots and overalls with black grease stripes on them. He'd been working on Popsicle, his giant diesel shovel.

"Thanks," said Du Pré to Bart.

Bart shrugged and he turned and he looked out the window at the Wolf Mountains.

Du Pré went outside and he got into his cruiser and he drove over to the gas tanks and he filled his car up. He checked the oil and the coolant.

He looked at the hose Simpson had put in his cruiser, it seemed a long damn time ago.

Du Pré picked up the little magic telephone. He dialed.

Rolly answered.

"That load you wanted," said Du Pré, "you be five miles maybe west of where we talk, I call you when it is ready."

Rolly broke the connection without another word.

"This be over soon," Du Pré murmured. His head ached a little and he felt his joints move with little stitches of pain. The day was damp.

I got the arthritis, too, Du Pré thought, don't seem so very long ago that I was a young guy, didn't have so much pains.

Du Pré totted up his broken bones, his bad sprains, the gunshot wound to the stomach. Just a surface wound, but the gun had been touching his shirt and pieces of the shirt and little blue flecks of powder and denim were stuck in his skin forever by the blast.

Cows, they kick me a lot, horses throw me, then, they get concerned, come back, stand on me while I am unconscious. Hope that I am all right.

I am grandfather. A bunch of times.

Little Gabriel Dumont, poor Louis Riel's general, him, his wife, they have no children. Gabriel, him very sad about that, but he take all the Métis for his, he take care of them. After the priests betray poor Louis and the English hang him, Gabriel come down here. He never speak to them priests again. He is buried, unmarked grave, down on the Musselshell.

Me, I want an unmarked grave, thought Du Pré.

That Du Pré, he is buried out there, we don't know. That Du Pré, he did what he had to.

Du Pré got in his old cruiser and he drove over to Benetsee's shack. There was a thin tendril of blue-gray smoke coming out of the rusty stovepipe and the front door of the cabin was open.

Du Pré got out and he went up the rickety steps to the little porch. There was firewood piled on both sides. The path to the door was thick with wood chips and the early yellow leaves from the cottonwoods near the creek.

Got that first frost, Du Pré thought.

Winter.

Young-Man-Who-Has-No-Name was sitting at the table, writing a letter. He wrote swiftly and gracefully. Du Pré could see, even upside down, that his script was lovely.

"Good morning," said the young man.

"Uh," said Du Pré. "You hear from that Benetsee?"

"Yes," said the young man. "He said to tell you you do very well. He is proud of you."

Du Pré nodded. Hearing that felt very good.

"That all?" said Du Pré.

The young man nodded. He went back to his letter.

Du Pré left. He drove over to the little highway that skirted the west end of the Wolfs and he headed up the road to the north. Many of the trees and the weeds in the roadside ditches had begun to turn color. The aspens were bright orange, always the first trees to turn. Flocks of common blackbirds whirled in the sky, hundreds at a time, gathering for the move south.

Them hummingbirds, they are already gone, Du Pré thought.

We don't got much of anything but winter up here.

It was getting on to dusk. Du Pré pulled off beside the road and he opened his cooler and he took out some sandwiches and a plastic container of potato salad. He ate and he drank cold tea.

He reached under the seat and took out a tracking unit, set it on the dashboard and switched it on. Nothing.

That Simpson don't come down this way he went to Miles City, hunting that girl in the choir, and Harvey has a couple people on that, Du Pré thought. But I don't think he do that. I think that that Simpson, he come down straight now. He will come here, maybe 10 P.M.

Du Pré slipped the fifth of whiskey out from under the seat and he had a slug and he rolled a smoke and then he started the cruiser and he got back on the old road and he headed north. The little highway that stobbed down from Canada to hit Highway 2 was perhaps twenty miles east of the campground at Raster Creek.

He got to come down that way, turn left, turn right, Du Pré thought.

One or the other.

The little highway ended at Raster Creek. Du Pré put the cruiser out of sight behind a screen of alders and he waited. He rolled a smoke and he got out and he wandered over the empty parking lot. A couple of semis barreled past, headed west. A pickup truck. Not much traffic this night.

He sipped a little whiskey. He watched the stars. He glanced, from time to time, at the tracking unit on the dashboard.

Suddenly, the green dot appeared, headed south on the little road from Canada. The liquid crystal display read 47 miles. Du Pré watched the dot. It was coming south. Simpson was traveling at a good rate.

When he got to the T-junction, he turned right. Headed west. Right for Du Pré.

Du Pré started the cruiser. He waited until Simpson was five miles away and then he drove out on the highway and he parked by the entrance to the rest stop. He reached under the backseat and he took out a flare and when the tracking unit said Simpson was a mile away he lit the flare and he dropped it on the road.

And now we pray no fucking cop comes along, Du Pré thought. Du Pré hunkered down out of sight and he racked a round into the chamber of his 9mm and he waited. He could see the light from Simpson's headlights on the top of the closest hill.

Simpson slowed down and moved out on the center line. He crept up to the flare and pulled in behind Du Pré's cruiser and he stopped and his door opened.

He stepped out.

He walked forward.

Du Pré stood up. He leveled the 9mm at Simpson, who was only fifteen feet away.

"Ho, Simpson," said Du Pré, "I kill you now, you know. You killed little Barbara Morissette, eh? Kill a lot of others. All up, down the highway, Texas to here."

Simpson froze. He said nothing.

Du Pré walked forward.

"You're crazy," said Simpson.

"Maybe I look, your van," said Du Pré. "Got little knives, stainless steel, black plastic handles? Little box, got earrings, maybe? Watches? Pieces of skin?"

Simpson was looking steadily at Du Pré.

"Let's look, your van," said Du Pré. He waved his gun and Simpson backed up toward the open door of his van.

"Let's look maybe," said Du Pré.

Du Pré's finger tripped the magazine release on his pistol. The magazine popped out and it landed on the asphalt with a metallic thump.

Simpson dived into his van and he slammed it into drive and he drove straight at Du Pré. Du Pré rolled away, toward the barrow pit.

Simpson swerved and he headed west, the van accelerating rapidly.

Du Pré watched the van crest the next hill.

He bent down and he picked up the magazine.

He put it back in the gun.

He picked up the burning flare and he carried it to the barrow pit and he doused it in a puddle.

A bright yellow light flared up to the west.

Du Pré heard a distant explosion.

He nodded and he got in his cruiser and he drove south toward home. When he got to the dirt road that led out to the pishkun he turned off and drove very slowly, the headlights throwing the rocks sticking up out of the thin soil into high relief.

It took the better part of an hour for Du Pré to grind up to the base of the tall cliff. He took the tracking unit and he scrambled up the steep trail to the top. He took the little black box apart and he dropped the pieces down rock fissures. Someday the ice would tear the rocks away from the cliff face. Some day, long time. He kept the batteries.

Du Pré took the whiskey out of his jacket pocket and he had some and he rolled a smoke and he looked up at the stars and then he looked out to the west where the plains rolled on, dark red and black, with pale blotches where the grass was thick.

Long time, Du Pré thought, some people say this was a sea, went all the way from the Arctic Ocean to the Gulf of Mexico.

Long time.

Du Pré felt the rock he was sitting on get colder. He stood up and he walked around till his butt wasn't so chilled.

Long time.

Du Pré felt very tired.

He struggled back down the trail and he got in his cruiser and he sat there for a while, smoking and drinking. There was enough water in the air to dew. It was damp and chilly out.

Du Pré took his bedroll out of the trunk and he carried it to a patch of thick grass by a dead spring.

He slept a long time.

The sun's heat brought him awake.

He stood up and he walked a couple steps and he pissed.

He stretched and yawned.

The plains went on west forever.

❧ CHAPTER 38 ❧

Du Pré looked at the crumpled burnt van. It had been crushed and then the gas tank had exploded and some of the glass that had stayed in the frames had melted to globs.

Harvey Wallace and Pidgeon were standing near the wrecked semi. It had flipped about three hundred yards away and the cab had been flattened down to the doorline. The trailer was on its side.

Du Pré walked over toward Harvey and Pidgeon.

Harvey glared at Du Pré and he walked away quickly.

Pidgeon looked at Du Pré for a long moment.

"Rolly was alive," she said. "They flew him out. Where he is, I don't know."

Du Pré nodded. I lie to Rolly, I kill the one who killed his little sister. But the only two know that are me and maybe Pidgeon, and now, who cares?

"Harvey'll get over it," said Pidgeon. "He's just ticked. He's sure you set this up but, of course, no way to prove it."

Du Pré shrugged.

A wrecker with a lowboy tilt-trailer behind pulled off the highway and it bounced over the ground to the smashed van. The driver backed the trailer up and he got out and put a cable on the van and he set the trailer bed down and he began to winch the burned hulk up onto the oak planks.

"Go through that with a very fine comb," said Pidgeon. "I expect we will find a few things. Simpson, and I don't know how, was alive enough to have started to crawl out when the fire started. He burned to death."

Du Pré nodded.

Good. Hope it hurt bad.

"Now," said Pidgeon, "I expect there will be just two hundred and some odd murder cases open forever. We won't ever really know. Thing about it is, you talk to these bastards, you never really know either. They ain't human, Du Pré. I don't know what they are."

Pidgeon took a filter cigarette from a pigskin case and she lit it. The little breeze ruffled her long auburn hair.

An accident records van pulled up and technicians got out and began to walk back up the highway, looking for the black skid marks.

"You be around some?" said Du Pré.

Pidgeon shook her head. "Got some charmer down in Alabama who skins his victims. Alive. Got another in western Pennsylvania, strangles and then beheads. Got a lot of them, Du Pré. This is over. And, it's never over. Harvey and me, we'll stop in Toussaint on our way down to Billings, but not for long. It's what we do, you know."

Du Pré nodded.

"Harvey's calmed down some," said Pidgeon. "I can tell by the way he stands. You want to talk to him, maybe it's a good time."

Du Pré glanced over at Harvey, who had his hands in his pockets. He was looking off in the far distance.

He walked over and stood by his friend.

Harvey glanced at him and went on looking far away.

"Pidgeon say you maybe stop in Toussaint, your way back," said Du Pré.

"Yeah," said Harvey.

"Well," said Du Pré. "I think I go, maybe, we have something to eat you get there."

"We will," sighed Harvey. "Du Pré, just keep your fucking mouth shut, will you?"

He went back to looking far off.

Du Pré turned his cruiser around and he headed back to Toussaint. It was late afternoon when he got there. The bar had several trucks and cars parked in front of it.

Du Pré went in.

Benny Klein was standing at the bar, having a beer. Susan was pulling a draft pitcher for a couple cowboys.

Du Pré walked up and he stood next to Benny.

"Afternoon," said Benny, twinkling. "Heard about some wreck up on the Hi-Line. You know anything?"

"Semi hit this van," said Du Pré.

"Messy," said Benny.

Madelaine came out of the women's john.

Du Pré looked at her.

He nodded, once.

Madelaine smiled. She smiled and her white teeth shone. She came to Du Pré and she put her arms around him and she hugged him swaying a little.

"Come sit," she said. "I get you a drink." She went behind the bar.

Du Pré saw her beaded purse on one of the little tables by the far wall. He went and sat with his back to the room.

"That Lourdes she will be back in two days," said Madelaine. "She like that Chicago. I talk to Bart's Aunt Marella. She is a good lady. She said Bart, he thinks she is his maiden aunt but he is so drunk both times that she is married he don't remember. She got two daughters, one about Lourdes's age. Bart, he don't remember they are his cousins."

"Yah," said Du Pré. "Well, that Bart he drink some there for some long time, you know."

"It is over, yes?" said Madelaine.

Du Pré nodded.

"Du Pré," said Madelaine, "you drink some whiskey, we eat some food, you get your fiddle and make some music. It is our life, yes."

Du Pré drank a little. Madelaine dragged him out to the dance floor and she danced and then Du Pré did, too. There were a couple good dance tunes on the jukebox, a record Du Pré had brought from Canada.

They danced to "Boiling Cabbage." They danced heel and toe to "The Water Road."

Susan Klein brought Du Pré a big steak and some more whiskey.

Du Pré ate like a pig.

Madelaine leaned over and she smiled.

"You that," she said. "My babies they are safe now."

The bar filled up.

Bassman showed up and some more of Du Pré's cousins from Canada and from Turtle Mountain, the old Red River country. There were maybe ten good musicians and they all played, sitting in and leaving, dancing and drinking.

Du Pré stopped fiddling for a minute and he went to the john and he came back out and he ran right in to Benetsee, who was standing at the back of the crowd with Young-Man-Who-Has-No-Name.

The old man was as solid as a tree trunk rooted in earth.

Du Pré grabbed his shoulder and he turned him around.

Benetsee was laughing.

"You old bastard," said Du Pré, "what are you here now for, eh?"

"Come in, drink some wine," said Benetsee, his black eyes laughing, "You got some tobacco? Some manners?"

Du Pré nodded and he rolled a thick smoke for the old man.

He lit the cigarette and he passed it to Benetsee.

"Pret' good," the old man said.

He smoked happily.

Susan Klein brought him a beer mug full of the awful cheap white wine that he liked. She kissed him on the cheek.

"Damn," said Benetsee. "Wine, pretty women they are kissing me. I like this place."

Young-Man-Who-Has-No-Name laughed.

"I call this one 'Pelon' now," said Benetsee.

"What him call him?" said Du Pré.

"I don't care," said Benetsee.

"Pelon," said the young man.

"I got to talk, you," said Du Pré.

Benetsee shook his head.

"We sweat some soon," he said. "I am here, drink wine, kiss pretty women, and maybe I play the flute."

Du Pré nodded.

He went back up and he fiddled with Bassman and some guitar pickers and a guy he didn't know who played pret' good accordion.

Pidgeon and Harvey came in and they stood by the door. When Du Pré looked at them Pidgeon tossed her head a little.

Du Pré finished the song and he stepped down from the little stage and he made his way through the crowd to them. Pidgeon and Harvey went outside and Du Pré followed.

It was cool and pleasant out in the night air. It was very hot in the bar.

"We're on our way," said Pidgeon. "Just wanted to say hello."

Harvey stood there.

"Challis is in the hospital in Billings," said Pidgeon. "He was hurt pretty badly. They had to take out his spleen and he had a collapsed lung, some fractures, pretty smashed up."

"OK," said Du Pré.

"It's been real nice," said Pidgeon. She shook hands with Du Pré.

Du Pré turned to Harvey.

Harvey hit him, hard, in the jaw.

Du Pré flew over the handrail and he landed on his head in the dirt.

He struggled to his feet.

"Don't fuck with me again," said Harvey.

"Harvey!" said Pidgeon.

They walked off to a tan government pool car.

Du Pré sat up. He rubbed his jaw.

He looked up. Madelaine was standing there.

She put her hand to her mouth and she ululated.

Victory's song.

Harvey drove off without looking back.

Du Pré and Madelaine waved anyway.

✤ CHAPTER 39 ✤

Du Pré stopped for a minute in the parking lot of the hospital. He looked up at the blank glass windows and he shook his head and he went on. Madelaine held his arm tighter.

She pulled him to a halt fifty feet from the front doors.

"Your wife die here, Du Pré," she said. "Old hurts, they leave scars. It is all right. I love you."

Du Pré looked at her a moment. She know what is bothering me, he thought, when I do not know.

He smiled a little and he nodded. They went on in.

The front desk clerk directed them toward the right floor.

"Critical care may not let you see him," the clerk said. "I can call for you."

Du Pré nodded. He walked Madelaine around in a circle while they waited.

"You can go up," said the clerk, "but they may ask you to leave if they feel the patient is tiring or getting agitated."

Du Pré and Madelaine went to the elevator and up to the floor. The doors opened and the smell of illness and disinfectants surrounded them.

Du Pré winced. Madelaine gripped his arm a little harder.

A nurse led them down to Rolly's room. She opened the door very gently, putting out a hand to make Du Pré and Madelaine wait. She went in very quietly.

They heard her voice, then Rolly's, strong and deep.

She came back out and motioned them to go on in.

Rolly was propped up on pillows, the bed cranked high. His head was a turban of bandages and a weight hung off a frame at the foot of the bed, a cable running to the end of a cast.

His left arm was gone.

But his blue eyes twinkled out of his swollen face. Purple, green, and black bruises lay across all his skin. The bridge of his nose had a metal form taped to it.

"Mr. Du Pré and Miss Madelaine," said Rolly, laughing. "Ain't this some shit? I need a jukebox and a barstool and a beer. Pool table ain't so much of a concern anymore, I guess."

"You like pool?" said Du Pré.

"Can't remember," said Rolly. "It was a long damn time ago."

Rolly handed a note to Du Pré. His right hand had a patch of adhesive across the back of it. Du Pré unfolded the note.

"Be careful, the cops have been here some and the flowers ain't mine."

Du Pré nudged Madelaine and she glanced at the note and then at Rolly and she nodded.

"How long you be here?" said Du Pré.

"Couple weeks," said Rolly. "Got to come back, get fitted for an arm. You know, they got ones now that are part electronic. What they call 'em, bionic?"

Du Pré shrugged. He watched very little television.

"What else they cut off?" said Madelaine.

"Just the arm," said Rolly. "They thought about cutting off the leg but I told 'em I'd have to kill 'em."

"Hmm," said Madelaine. "After you get out of here where you go? You be a while, getting better, you know."

"Uh," said Rolly, "Well, your pal Bart called and he give me a choice, go someplace or come up to Toussaint and get to know Booger Tom and him better. So I guess that's what I'll do."

"Ah," said Madelaine.

"Good," said Du Pré. "She have someone, put that good soup down. Fuss over. Me, I am scared to death I get sick."

"What is wrong, my soup?" said Madelaine.

"Not enough salt," said Du Pré.

"Salt's bad, your heart," said Madelaine.

"These days," Rolly laughed, "If it tastes good at all, it's downright toxic."

Du Pré nodded and laughed.

"You need us, do anything?" said Madelaine.

Rolly grinned. "Know any hookers wear nurse's uniforms?" he said.

Du Pré laughed.

"OK," said Madelaine. "Anything else?"

"All I got to do is wait and sleep," said Rolly. "I rode a long ways on a big horse."

Madelaine tugged a flat pint of whiskey out of her purse and she showed it to Rolly. He held out his hand. She gave it to him and he slipped it under the bedclothes.

The nurse who had shown them in opened the door.

"Five minutes," she said. "He has a doctor coming."

She shut the door.

Madelaine got a small oblong plastic pill container from her purse, the sort that has seven compartments. She went to the sink and she ran a thin stream of water and she grabbed several paper towels from the dispenser as she moved the box back and forth under the stream. She dumped out the excess.

She went and sat on the bed and she put her forefinger into the paint and she lifted it up and put a crimson slash on each side of his mouth. She put black and yellow in zigzags on his cheeks. A stripe of blue from his lower lip down under his chin.

Madelaine nodded. She took out a mirror and she held it up to Rolly, and he looked at himself and he nodded.

"Thank you," he said.

"OK," said Du Pré. "We see you, Toussaint."

Rolly stuck his thumb up.

They all laughed.

Madelaine and Du Pré made good time to the elevator, getting in

190

just as the doors closed. They were walking across the parking lot in a matter of two or three minutes.

"That damn nurse she shit rusty pickles she see him," said Du Pré.

"Yah," said Madelaine. "Me, I want a beer."

Du Pré looked at her. She didn't drink beer very often. Very hot days and this was a cool one.

They got into the old cruiser and Madelaine pointed downtown and Du Pré nodded and he drove down to the poor part of Billings, where the Indians on drunks and the hobos and the mentally ill pushed their homes in shopping carts down the pitted sidewalks.

"There," said Madelaine, pointing at a shabby sign above a little bar. The windows were glazed with dirt. A wino was sleeping curled up in the stairwell next to the front door.

Du Pré laughed.

So did Madelaine.

"Maybe I ask you a better place, start looking for Rolly's hooker," said Madelaine. "You, know them probably, yes?"

"Oh, yes," said Du Pré. "Me, I spend much time here, you bet."

They got out and they went into the bar. A very tired-looking middle-aged woman was slumped on a stool behind the bar, a cigarette hanging from her lip. She was watching a soap opera on the little television on a shelf behind her.

Du Pré ordered bottle beers for both of them. He went off to the john to take a leak. The floor was swimming in water from a broken seal at the base of the toilet. Du Pré used the toilet anyway.

By the time he came back out Madelaine was talking into the telephone on the bar. The woman behind the bar looked cheerful.

Spread a little money around, Du Pré thought, it is like the sun.

Madelaine turned away from Du Pré when he slid back up on the barstool. She listened for another moment.

"Yah, well," she said. "You do this, hundred up front, another you come back with a note from him, uh?"

Madelaine put the phone back in the cradle.

They drank beer for a half hour.

A good-looking hooker came in and she walked right up to Madelaine.

Madelaine nodded. The hooker was wearing a crisp nurse's uniform.

"Four forty-two," said Madelaine, handing her a hundred-dollar bill.

The hooker went out.

"This soap all right with you?" said the woman behind the bar. She smiled. Her false teeth had clots of dental fixative on them.

"Yah," said Madelaine.

Du Pré laughed.

They got some fives and they went to the video poker machines. The machines were shut off.

They went back to the bar and sat and a man in a workman's uniform came in and he carted the machines out the door.

The woman behind the bar never looked away from the television as the four machines went out the door.

Du Pré looked at Madelaine. He grinned. They both laughed.

An actress on the television was suffering from amnesia.

A commercial sold soap. Another, feminine hygiene.

Madelaine reached down and took Du Pré's hand and she squeezed his fingers.

They had another bottle of beer each.

The hooker in the nurse's uniform came in.

She handed Madelaine a slip of paper.

Madelaine glanced at it and she laughed and she handed over another hundred-dollar bill.

She gave the note to Du Pré.

"Ahhhhhhhhhhhhhh. Paint a great hit. Raster Creek," Du Pré read.

"We go home now," said Madelaine.

✤ CHAPTER 40 ✤

Du Pré was fiddling and Bassman and Père Godin were backing him up. Père Godin was famous for having been thrown out of a seminary in Quebec when three very pregnant young women accused him of fathering their impending children. He was in his late seventies now and he had fathered more than forty children. He played the accordion and he sang in a high falsetto, a tenor, a baritone, a bass. Double-voiced. Du Pré had never heard anyone else like him.

The Toussaint Bar was packed. There were local people and then many from Turtle Mountain and from Canada. The women wore bright dresses with beadings and bells, the men ribbon shirts.

Godin quavered to the end of the ballad and Bassman and Du Pré quickly finished. It was time for a break.

Du Pré was sweating in the heavy silk shirt that Madelaine had made for him.

He made his way over to her and he put an arm around her. She grinned and looked merrily up at him. Her face was a little flushed. She had been drinking her sweet pink wine.

"I never see so many Métis, one place, here," said Du Pré. There were about thirty in the room. One couple had come from Manitoba, a drive of nearly a thousand miles from their home.

"Why they here?" said Du Pré.

"Listen to my Du Pré fiddle," said Madelaine. "You are a very famous man, you know, them records you made, people listen to them."

Du Pré nodded.

Bullshit, he thought. They got plenty good fiddlers, Turtle Moun-

193

tain, Manitoba, Alberta. Me, I am OK, not the best. Me, I do not want ever to be the best, anything I do. Does bad things to you, that best.

"That Père Godin, he have what, fifty children?" said Du Pré. "I hear he just had twins, latest wife."

"Ah, yes," said Madelaine. "He is very charming man I hear. One, my cousins, Canada, she have one of his."

Bassman was leaned up on one hand against the wall, talking to a pretty woman in a turquoise velvet dress, who was not his wife. His wife was home, swelling with child. Bassman and the woman went out.

Some of that grass, thought Du Pré, these musicians are some playboys. Good hearts, lots of damage, them good hearts.

Somebody handed Du Pré a glass of whiskey and water and ice. He drank thirstily. Playing made him burn. Tomorrow he would be exhausted.

Susan Klein bustled past. "What's the occasion?" she said. "I'm damn near out of some of my booze."

Du Pré put one palm up and he shrugged.

"Ver' charming man," said Madelaine. "Père Godin, he is some guy. There are some guys, Du Pré, that women just cannot get mad at. They are born, that. He is one of them."

Du Pré looked at the silver-haired old fart. He was fairly tall and rail-thin and he had big hands with very long tapered fingers.

"We go maybe outside," said Madelaine. "It is plenty hot in here."

They struggled to the door and went out into the cool night. There was no cloud or moon and the stars burned in the velvet black sky.

"Wheh!" said Madelaine. "This is some better!"

Du Pré felt the silk cold on his back where the little wind from the west was touching lightly. His neck itched. He took off the silk bandanna wound around it.

Ahh, he thought, I don't put it back on neither.

"I don't see Bart," said Du Pré.

"He come later," said Madelaine, "I talk to him, he will be along, probably a few minutes."

194

Du Pré nodded. Bart was so shy, really, that Du Pré couldn't re-member him in any crowd.

Booger Tom was pissing in the shadow of a cottonwood in the little park across the road.

Du Pré looked down the street. One of Bart's Rovers was coming on, the big SUV pulled up and the rear window rolled down.

"Evenin'," said Rolly Challis. Bart got out and he went to the back of the rig and he opened it and he took down a wheelchair and he unfolded it and snapped the pressure rings together.

Bart wheeled the chair up to the door and it opened and Rolly swung his leg out and Du Pré went to help Bart lower him into the chair. Bart pushed the wheelchair over to the steps that led up to the front door of the bar and Du Pré got on one side and Bart the other and they lifted the chair up to the boardwalk and then Du Pré pushed Rolly on in while Bart went to park his rig.

Père Godin came and he cleared the way for Rolly's chair and Du Pré wheeled him up right next to the tiny stage. Susan Klein brought Rolly a big glass of whiskey. Rolly took tobacco and papers from his shirt pocket and he rolled a smoke expertly and he licked the paper and tucked it in his mouth.

Madelaine lit the cigarette for him.

Oh, Du Pré thought, now I am knowing why all of this.

Père Godin got up on the stage and he lifted the heavy accordion up and he shrugged into the harness and he checked it for tune. Bassman stepped up on the stage and he picked up his fretless elec-tric bass and he put the strap on and he turned toward his amplifier and he ran a quick scale and then he bent and fiddled with the knobs.

Du Pré kissed Madelaine and he stepped up and he picked up his fiddle and he plucked the strings with his left forefinger and listened close to the harmonics. He twisted the peg for a string that had gone a little flat.

A Métis that Du Pré didn't know stepped up and he lifted a flat Celtic drum over his head and he began to beat on it with the stick, a fast rhythm with backbeats. Père Godin chuffed the accordion in time. Bassman did stops on his bass.

Du Pré nodded and he ripped off some icy little notes.

"Salteux!" screamed Père Godin.

One of the Métis war songs. The victory song.

Salteux, the Métis warriors, and this for the Salteur Du Pré and the Salteur Challis.

The Métis roared.

The ranch folk backed away and the Métis women went to the space in the center of the floor and they began to dance. They ululated, hands to mouths, while they bobbed, legs pumping. The floor shook. The many voices warbling the ululations blended, rose and fell.

Père Godin broke into riffs of reedy chords and notes not on the European scales.

Du Pré fiddled. He played notes from his blood. Smoke. Buffalo on the shortgrass prairie.

The Salteux had run the Sioux out of the Great Lakes country and the Cheyennes out of Wisconsin.

Du Pré fiddled between his two worlds of the blood.

He looked down at Madelaine.

Her eyes flashed crimson fire, so did her hair when the light struck just right.

Your babies are safe, Du Pré thought.